THE THIRD READER

READING-LITERATURE
THIRD READER

BY

HARRIETTE TAYLOR TREADWELL

AND

MARGARET FREE

ILLUSTRATED BY

FREDRICK RICHARDSON

YESTERDAY'S CLASSICS

CHAPEL HILL, NORTH CAROLINA

Cover and arrangement © 2008 Yesterday's Classics, LLC.

This edition, first published in 2008 by Yesterday's Classics, an imprint of Yesterday's Classics, LLC, is an unabridged republication of the work originally published by Row, Peterson and Company in 1912. For the complete listing of the books that are published by Yesterday's Classics, please visit www.yesterdaysclassics.com. Yesterday's Classics is the publishing arm of the Baldwin Online Children's Literature Project which presents the complete text of hundreds of classic books for children at www.mainlesson.com.

ISBN-10: 1-59915-267-3

ISBN-13: 978-1-59915-267-7

Yesterday's Classics, LLC
PO Box 3418
Chapel Hill, NC 27515

PURPOSE AND PLAN

THOSE who have examined this book, together with the Primer and First and Second Readers, should have no difficulty in apprehending the purpose of the series,— to train children in reading and appreciating literature through *reading literature*.

The Primer contains nine of the best folk tales, true to the original, and yet written in such a simple style that children can begin reading the *real story* during the first week in school. The First Reader contains thirteen similar stories, of gradually increasing difficulty, and thirty-three of the best rhymes and jingles suitable for young children. This constitutes a *course in literature*, twenty-two stories and thirty-three child poems, as well adapted to first-grade children as are the selections for "college entrance requirements" to high-school students.

The Second Reader introduces fables and fairy stories and continues folk tales and simple poems. Others have used some of the same material in readers, but in a quite different way. Their purpose seems to have been to "mix thoroughly." We have organized the material: a group of fables, several groups of folk and fairy stories, a group of Mother Goose, of Rossetti, of

Stevenson, and so on; so that the child may get a body, not a mere bit, of one kind of material before passing to another. Thus from the first he is trained to associate related literature and to organize what he reads.

The transition to this Third Reader will be found easy and to accord with the normal interests of the children. In prose the folk and fairy story is retained, but is merged into the wonder tale, which becomes a dominant note, while the fable gives place to more extended and more modern animal stories. The poetry begins with the group from Stevenson, whom the children have already learned to enjoy. Then follow selections from Lydia Maria Child, Lucy Larcom, Eugene Field, and a score of others dealing mainly with children's interests in animals and other forms of nature.

With these books, besides merely learning to read, the child has the joy of reading the *best in the language*, and he is forming his taste for all subsequent reading. This development of taste should be recognized and encouraged. From time to time the children should be asked to choose what they would like to re-read as a class, or individuals who read well aloud may be asked to select something already studied to read to the others. This kind of work gives the teacher opportunity to find out what is in a selection that the children like, and to commend what seems to her best.

The fact that some children voluntarily memorize a story or a poem should have hearty approval. It shows abiding interest and enjoyment, and it is likely to give, for the young child at least, the maximum of *literary saturation.*

The authors and publishers gratefully acknowledge permission of Charles Scribner's Sons to reprint the three selections from Eugene Field's "Poems of Childhood."

—The Authors.

CONTENTS

The Enchanted Horse....................1

Aladdin and His Lamp..................12

Sinbad the Sailor.....................27

Group of Robert Louis Stevenson's Poems

    The Land of Nod....................31

    Foreign Lands......................32

    The Land of Counterpane............34

    Marching Song......................35

    The Land of Storybooks.............36

    Foreign Children...................38

    The Wind...........................39

    The Lamplighter....................40

    From a Railway Carriage............42

The Ugly Duckling.....................43

GROUP OF LYDIA MARIA CHILD'S POEMS
- Thanksgiving Day .57
- Who Stole the Bird's Nest? 59

THE BEAR AND THE FOX .63
THE FOX AND THE WOLF. 69
THE MAN AND THE SERPENT 73
THE FOX AS HERDSMAN. 77

GROUP OF LUCY LARCOM'S POEMS
- The Brown Thrush 80
- Berrying Song 82
- Little Nannie 83
- Calling the Violet 85
- If I Were a Sunbeam 88

ALICE IN WONDERLAND 89

GROUP OF EUGENE FIELD'S POEMS
- Wynken, Blynken, and Nod 109
- The Shut-Eye Train 112
- The Duel. 115

The Snow-Image	117
A Visit from St. Nicholas	133
A Dog of Flanders	139
Group of Miscellaneous Poems	
Robin Redbreast	148
Little Gustava	150
Good Night and Good Morning	152
How Doth the Little Busy Bee	154
The Bluebird	155
Answer to a Child's Question	156
Black Beauty	157
Ginger	167
Group of Humorous Poems	
The Spider and the Fly	181
The Owl and the Pussy-Cat	185
A Lobster Quadrille	187
The Mountain and the Squirrel	189
Tom the Chimney-Sweep	190
Tom the Water-Baby	201

Tom Becomes a Man 223

Group of Miscellaneous Poems

    A Boy's Song 237

    How the Leaves Came Down 239

    Sweet and Low 241

    September 242

    The Wonderful World.............. 243

    The Throstle..................... 244

    The Sea 245

    Ariel's Song..................... 246

    Prayer 246

The Enchanted Horse

In far away Persia the sultan held great feasts on the first day of the year. To one of these feasts came a Hindu with a wooden horse. It was so well made that it looked in every way like a real horse.

The Hindu threw himself upon his face before the throne, and said, "This horse is a wonder. If I mount my horse and wish myself in any part of the earth, in a short time I find myself there. If your majesty command me, I will show you this wonder."

The sultan, who was fond of anything curious, bade the Hindu show what he could do. The Hindu put his foot into the stirrup, mounted the horse, and asked the sultan to command him.

"Ride to yonder mountain," said the sultan, "and bring me a branch of the palm tree that grows at the foot of the hill."

The Hindu turned a peg that was in the hollow of the horse's neck. The horse rose from the ground and carried his rider through the air with the speed of the wind. In a few minutes the man returned with the palm branch and laid it at the feet of the sultan. The sultan was filled with wonder and wished to have the horse.

"Sire," said the Hindu, "I will not part with my horse unless I receive the hand of your fair daughter as my bride. This is the only bargain I can make with you."

The people laughed at this proposal, and the prince was very angry. "Father," he said, "I hope you will consider that an insult."

"Son," said the sultan, "I will not give him my daughter, but before I bargain with him try the horse yourself and tell me what you think of it."

The Hindu was delighted to have the prince try the horse. He ran before the prince to help him mount the horse, and to show him how to guide it. But the prince mounted the wonderful horse without waiting for the Hindu to help him. He turned the peg which he had seen the Hindu use. Instantly the horse rose into the air and they were soon out of sight.

The Hindu was alarmed. He threw himself at the feet of the sultan and cried, "Sire, your majesty saw that the horse flew away so rapidly I could not tell the prince the secret of bringing him back. Let us hope that he will find the peg which will do so."

The sultan saw the danger for his son. "May he not land on a rock or in the sea?" he asked the Hindu.

"No," replied the Hindu. "The horse will go where he wishes, and he will wish to land in a place of safety."

"Your head shall answer for my son's life if he does not return," said the sultan. He then ordered his officers to throw the Hindu into prison.

In the meantime the prince was carried into the air, higher and higher. At last he rose so high he could not see the earth. It was then he began to think about returning. He turned the peg the other way, but to his horror he found that the horse rose still higher. Then he remembered he had not waited to learn how to descend. He examined the horse's head and neck, and found a small peg behind his ear. He turned this peg and soon found that he was slowly descending.

It was dark and he did not know where he was going, but he wished he would

land in a place of safety. When the horse alighted he found himself on the roof of a grand palace. He looked about and saw a bright light shining through the curtains. He listened. All was quiet. He pulled a curtain aside and stepped in.

There on a couch lay the most beautiful maiden he had ever seen. He fell on his knees beside her and gently touched her sleeve. The princess opened her eyes and, seeing a handsome prince, was too surprised to speak.

The prince bowed low and said, "Beautiful princess, you see before you the son of the Sultan of Persia. I have had a wonderful adventure. Yesterday I was in my father's court, to-day I am in an unknown land and I pray for your protection."

"Take courage, prince," replied the princess, "hospitality is met with in our country as well as in Persia. I am the daughter of the Sultan of Bengal and I grant you the protection you ask. As you must be in need of food and rest I will order my servants to attend you."

The next morning the princess dressed herself with great care, and sent word to the prince that she would see him. He hastened to her. After thanking her he told her all about the enchanted horse. Then he said, "I must return to my father, the sultan."

The princess begged that he remain long enough to know something of the country.

The prince could not refuse the request and for many days there was great feasting. At last the prince saw that he must return to his home. He then begged the princess to go back to Persia with him as his bride.

The next morning they went to the roof of the palace. The prince turned the head of the horse toward Persia. He placed the princess behind him and turned the peg, and the horse once more mounted into the air. In a very short time they arrived at the capital of Persia.

The sultan was delighted to see his son again and consented to his marriage with the princess.

Then he sent for the Hindu and said, "My son has returned. Take your horse and be gone forever."

The Hindu was very angry and wished to be revenged. He mounted his horse and, snatching up the princess of Bengal, placed her behind him. Then he turned the peg and the horse rose into the air.

When the prince saw his beloved princess borne away on the enchanted horse he lost no time, but dressed himself as a dervish and started in search of her.

In the meantime the Hindu, with the princess, had arrived at the capital of Cashmere. He did not enter the city, but left the princess on a grassy spot in the woods and went to get her some food and drink. Hearing someone passing, the princess cried out for help. It was the

Sultan of Cashmere returning from the hunt. He heard the cries of the princess and went to her rescue.

The princess said, "I am a princess. This Hindu is a wicked magician who brought me here on an enchanted horse."

The sultan ordered the guard to bind the Hindu and throw him into prison. Then he took the princess to his palace. She thought, when she had told her story, that he would help her to return to Persia, but the sultan resolved to marry her himself the very next day.

At daybreak the princess was awakened by the sound of drums and bugles. The sultan soon arrived and informed her that it was a part of their marriage ceremony.

This filled the princess with horror and she pretended to go mad.

The sultan ordered the wedding to be put off until the princess was better. But the princess was too wise to get better.

The sultan sent for all the doctors in the country to cure her madness, but the princess flew at them in such a rage that they were afraid to go near her.

The prince of Persia heard of this princess who had gone mad, and of the enchanted horse. He decided it must be the princess of Bengal. He hastened to the kingdom of Cashmere dressed as a doctor. He went to the palace and declared he could cure the princess. The sultan had given up all hope, but he allowed the doctor to see the mad princess.

When he entered the room the princess turned to fly at him. But when she saw that it was her own dear prince she fell into his arms and wept for joy. Then she told him all that had happened, and that she had only pretended to go mad.

The prince went to the sultan and said, "There is only one way to cure the princess. Some of the magic from the enchanted horse has entered into her. She must be set on the horse's back, a fire lighted around her and an incense burned in the flames. I promise you that the princess will be completely cured in a few minutes."

The next day the enchanted horse was brought into the open square. A great crowd of people gathered to see the wonderful cure. The sultan and his court were in the gallery which was built for the occasion.

The princess, dressed in a fine robe and covered with jewels, was placed on the horse. The fire was lighted and some incense thrown into it. Soon a dense cloud of smoke surrounded the princess so that she could not be seen. The prince jumped up behind her and turned the peg.

Just as the horse rose into the air the prince said, "Sultan, if you would marry a princess, you must first get her consent."

That same day they arrived in Persia, where they were married and lived happily ever after.

—Arabian Nights.

Aladdin and His Lamp

Aladdin lived with his mother in a large city of Persia. His father had been a tailor and had left them very poor.

One day when the lad was playing in the street a stranger passed by. This stranger was a magician from Africa. When he saw Aladdin he thought, "This boy will serve me." He asked the boy's companions about him and his father. Then, taking the boy aside, the stranger said, "Are you not the son of Mus-ta-pha the tailor?"

"I am, sir," said Aladdin, "but my father has been dead many years."

The stranger threw his arms around the lad and kissed him many times. "I am your uncle," he said. "Your father was my own brother. I have been out of the country and did not know of his death." He then gave Aladdin a handful of money and sent him home.

Aladdin ran home to his mother and, when he told her about it, she said, "Your father had a brother but he is dead."

The next day the magician found Aladdin again. This time he put two pieces of gold into his hand and said, "Carry this to your mother and tell her that I will come to see her to-night."

That night during supper the magician talked much of his brother and told Aladdin that he would take a shop for him. Then the widow believed that he was her husband's brother.

Next day the magician bought Aladdin a fine suit of clothes and took him all over the city. Then they went a long way into the country. At last they came to the mountains. The magician said, "Gather some sticks and I will kindle a fire and show you something wonderful."

Aladdin did as he was bid. Then the magician took some powder from his girdle, threw it on the fire, and said some magic words. The earth trembled and opened before them. And there lay a flat stone with a brass ring in the middle.

"Beneath this stone lies a treasure which is to be yours," said the magician, "but you must do just as I tell you."

Aladdin grasped the ring and, saying the names of his father and grandfather as he was told, he lifted the stone.

"At the bottom of these steps you will find a door," said the magician. "It will lead you into a place divided into three halls. In each of these halls you will see four large brass cisterns filled with gold and silver. But do not meddle with them. Above all things do not touch the walls with your clothes or you will die instantly. These halls lead into a garden of fine fruit. Walk on until you come to a lighted lamp set in a niche. Take the lamp down and bring it to me."

The magician then drew a ring from his finger and gave it to Aladdin. "It is a charm to guard against all evil," said he, "so long as you obey me."

Aladdin found everything just as the magician had said. He put the lamp in his waistband and started back. Going through the garden he noticed that on the trees were fruits of all colors. Some were white, some clear as crystal, some red, some green, some blue, some purple, and others yellow. The white were pearls, the crystal were diamonds, the red were rubies, the green were emeralds, the blue were turquoises, the purple were amethysts, and the yellow were ambers.

Aladdin loaded himself with all these riches and returned to the mouth of the cave. As soon as he saw the magician he cried out, "Pray, uncle, lend me your hand to help me out."

"Give me the lamp first," said the magician.

"I can not give it to you now," answered Aladdin, "but I will as soon as I am up."

The magician, who thought only of the lamp, said, "You must give me the lamp first."

And Aladdin, whose arms were full of the fruit, answered, "I can not give it to you unless you help me out first."

At this the magician flew into a passion. He threw some powder on the fire, said some magic words, and the stone rolled back into its place. When he saw he could not get the lamp, he left Persia and returned to Africa.

Aladdin remained in the cave without food or drink two days, crying and wondering what to do. At last he clasped his hands in prayer. In so doing, he rubbed the ring which the magician had given him. A great

genie rose out of the earth saying, "What would'st thou have? I am the slave of the ring and will obey thee in all things."

"Deliver me from this cave," cried Aladdin. Immediately the earth opened and Aladdin found himself outside. He went home to his mother, showed her the lamp and the colored fruit, and told her all that had happened. He was faint from hunger, but the widow had no money to buy food.

"I will go and sell the lamp and the money will buy us food for breakfast and dinner," said Aladdin.

His mother said, "The lamp is very dirty. If I clean it you can get more for it."

But no sooner had she begun to rub it than the genie of the lamp appeared and said, "What would'st thou have?"

"Bring us something to eat," said Aladdin boldly.

The genie disappeared and immediately returned with a silver plate full of rich meats, two silver cups, and two bottles of wine.

Thus Aladdin and his mother lived for many years.

One day the Sultan ordered that every one was to stay at home and close his shutters while the princess passed by.

Aladdin was seized with a desire to see her face. So he peeped through the shutters. As the princess went by she lifted her veil, and Aladdin saw her face.

Then he went and told his mother that he loved the princess, and that he could not live without her. He begged her to go to the emperor and ask for his daughter in marriage. So, to please her son, the mother took some jewels for the emperor and set out, trusting in the lamp. She went every day for a week and stood in the same place before the emperor. The sixth day he called her to him and asked what she wanted. She knelt before the throne and told him of her son's love for the princess. Then she gave him the jewels.

The emperor was surprised to see so many large and beautiful jewels. He looked at them a long time. Then he exclaimed, "Is not this present worthy of the princess? Shall I not give her to the one who sends it?" Turning to the poor widow, he said, "Good woman, go home and tell your son that I can not marry the princess to any one for three months. At that time come again."

When the three months were over Aladdin again sent his mother to the emperor. He said, "Your son must first send me forty basins of gold brimful of jewels, carried by forty black slaves, led by forty white ones, all richly dressed."

"I would do more than that for the princess," answered her son when his mother told him the emperor's demand.

He called the genie and in a few moments forty black slaves and forty white ones set out for the palace, followed by Aladdin's mother. Entering the palace, they knelt before the emperor.

"Good morning," said the emperor, "return and tell your son I wait for him with open arms."

When the mother told Aladdin, he called his genie and said, "I want a fine robe, a white horse harnessed in gold and jewels, and twenty slaves to attend me. Beside this I want six white slaves to attend my mother, and ten thousand pieces of gold for the people along the streets."

It was no sooner said than done. When the emperor saw Aladdin, he came down

from his throne to meet him. He then led him into the hall, where a wedding feast was spread. The emperor intended to marry him to the princess that very day.

But Aladdin said, "I must first build a palace for the princess." He called his genie again and said, "Build me a palace of the finest marble set with jasper and agate and precious stones. In the center build me a great hall with a dome, whose walls must be of silver and gold. Each side must have six windows set with diamonds and rubies. There must be stables, and horses, and slaves, and a treasure house filled with gold and silver."

The next day the palace was finished. The princess said good-bye to her father and set out for Aladdin's palace. She was followed by a hundred slaves and a band of musicians. Four hundred pages with torchlights led the procession.

Aladdin met her and took her by the hand and led her into the great hall. The princess was charmed with him. After the wedding there was much feasting, singing and dancing.

Aladdin was always loving to his bride and generous to the people. Every time he went out he took two slaves to throw handfuls of money among them. He was made general of the army and won several battles. Thus he lived happily for several years.

By that time the magician in Africa had learned of the escape of Aladdin with the magic lamp. Immediately he set out for

Persia. When he reached the city he found that Aladdin had gone hunting for eight days. This gave him plenty of time. He bought a dozen copper lamps, put them into a basket and went to the palace crying, "New lamps for old ones."

The princess sent a slave to learn what the man was calling. Then she said, "There is an old lamp here which he may have."

Now this was Aladdin's magic lamp and the magician knew it was the one he wanted, because all the others were gold and silver. He took it eagerly and hurried out of the city.

When it became dark he drew the lamp from his breast and rubbed it. The genie appeared and the magician said, "I command thee to take me and the palace with all its people to Africa."

The next day the emperor looked out of the window toward the palace, and rubbed his eyes, for it was gone. Then he knew that all had been done by magic, and he flew into a great passion. He sent thirty men to bring Aladdin to him in chains. They met Aladdin riding home, bound him and carried him back to the emperor, who commanded him to be put into prison. At that the people, who loved Aladdin, raised a great cry and demanded that his life be spared.

Aladdin then begged for forty days in which to find the princess, and he said, "If in that time I do not find her, I will return for my punishment."

Aladdin's wish was granted and he went forth to find his bride. After three days of search he knelt down to pray. In doing so he rubbed the magic ring, and immediately the genie of the ring appeared. "What would'st thou have?" asked the genie.

"Save my life and bring my palace back," replied Aladdin.

"That is not in my power," said the genie. "I am only the slave of the ring. You must ask the slave of the lamp."

"Then," said Aladdin, "take me to the

palace and set me down under the window of the palace of the princess."

He at once found himself in Africa. The princess heard his call, she opened the window and Aladdin entered.

After shedding tears of joy, Aladdin asked about the old lamp. The princess told him that she had changed it for a new one, and that the next thing she knew she was in Africa. "The man who has the lamp is here," she said, "and wishes me to marry him. He said my father had beheaded you."

Aladdin then told her to order supper as soon as the man returned. Then he gave her a powder and told her to put it into the magician's cup. The princess did just as Aladdin had told her. The magician drank from the cup and fell from his chair. Then Aladdin rushed in, took the lamp from the magician's bosom and rubbed it. The genie appeared.

"I command you to get the palace back to Persia," said Aladdin.

The next morning the emperor looked out of the window. He rubbed his eyes in wonder, for there stood the palace as before.

After this Aladdin and the princess lived in peace. When the emperor died, Aladdin and the princess ruled together for many years.

—Arabian Nights.

Sinbad the Sailor

My father was a rich merchant of Persia and left me a fortune, which I quickly spent. I soon grew tired of an idle life, and my love for adventure made me take to the sea. I joined a company of merchants, and we fitted out a sailing vessel. We went from island to island buying and selling goods.

One day we landed on an island covered with trees, but we could see neither man nor beast. We walked about picking fruit and eating it. At last, growing tired, I sat down under a tree and fell asleep. I cannot tell how long I slept, but when I awoke the ship was gone.

I rushed to and fro and cried in my despair. I climbed a tall tree and gazed toward the sea, but I could see nothing except sky and water. Then I turned toward

the land and, in the distance, I saw a large white object.

I came down from the tree and set off for it as fast as I could. It was a great white ball, as smooth as ivory, and seemed fifty paces around. I went to the other side to see if there were an opening, but I found none.

All of a sudden the sky became dark, as if covered by a thick cloud. I looked up and saw a large bird flying toward me. I had heard sailors speak of a large bird called the roc. I crept close to the large white ball. The bird settled upon it and covered it with her wings. I now knew the ball was a roc's egg. Before me was one of the legs of the bird, which was as large as the trunk of a tree. I took off my turban and tied myself fast to the leg. I hoped the bird would carry me from this lonely island.

The next morning the bird flew off. It carried me so high that I could not see the earth. Then it came down so fast that I lost my senses. When I opened my eyes, I was in a deep valley surrounded by high mountains which reached into the clouds.

The mountains were so steep and rocky that I could not climb them. The valley was covered with dazzling diamonds of great size. I wandered about all day hunting a way to escape. When night came, I crept into a small cave and blocked the entrance with stones.

The next day something fell on the ground beside me. I looked and saw a large piece of raw meat. Then several more pieces rolled over the cliff. I soon understood this. Some merchants were throwing the meat from the rocks above.

This fell upon the sharp points of the diamonds, which stuck into it. Then, when the rocs carried the meat to their nests on the cliff, the merchants frightened them away and picked the diamonds from the meat. I watched this a little while. Then I thought of a way of escape.

I filled my wallet with the largest diamonds. Then I tied a large piece of meat to my back and lay down upon my face. I soon heard the flapping of wings, and a roc caught me up with the meat and carried me to his nest.

The merchants rushed to get the diamonds. They were much surprised to find me. I told them my story, showed them my diamonds, and gave them each one.

I stayed with the merchants till they were ready to go home. Then we traveled many days across high mountains until we came to the sea, where we set sail. At last we reached Persia, and I settled down to enjoy my riches.

—*Arabian Nights.*

The Land of Nod

From breakfast on through all the day,
At home among my friends I stay,
But every night I go abroad
Afar into the land of Nod.

All by myself I have to go,
With none to tell me what to do—
All alone beside the streams
And up the mountain sides of dreams.

The strangest things are there for me,
Both things to eat and things to see,
And many frightening sights abroad
Till morning in the land of Nod.

Try as I like to find the way,
I never can get back by day,
Nor can remember plain and clear
The curious music that I hear.

—Robert Louis Stevenson.

Foreign Lands

Up into the cherry tree
Who should climb but little me?
I held the trunk with both my hands
And looked abroad on foreign lands.

I saw the next door garden lie,
Adorned with flowers, before my eye,
And many pleasant places more
That I had never seen before.

I saw the dimpling river pass
And be the sky's blue looking-glass;
The dusty roads go up and down
With people tramping into town.

If I could find a higher tree
Farther and farther I should see,
To where the grown-up river slips
Into the sea among the ships,

To where the roads on either hand
Lead onward into fairy land,
Where all the children dine at five,
And all the playthings come alive.

—Robert Louis Stevenson.

The Land of Counterpane

When I was sick and lay a-bed,
I had two pillows at my head,
And all my toys beside me lay
To keep me happy all the day.

And sometimes for an hour or so
I watched my leaden soldiers go,
With different uniforms and drills,
Among the bed clothes, through the hills;

And sometimes sent my ships in fleets
All up and down among the sheets;
Or brought my trees and houses out,
And planted cities all about.

I was the giant great and still
That sits upon the pillow-hill,
And sees before him, dale and plain,
The pleasant land of counterpane.

—Robert Louis Stevenson.

Marching Song

Bring the comb and play upon it!
   Marching, here we come!
Willie cocks his highland bonnet,
   Johnnie beats the drum.

Mary Jane commands the party,
   Peter leads the rear;
Feet in time, alert and hearty,
   Each a Grenadier!

All in the most martial manner
   Marching double-quick;
While the napkin like a banner
   Waves upon the stick!

Here's enough of fame and pillage.
   Great commander Jane!
Now that we've been round the
     village,
   Let's go home again.

—Robert Louis Stevenson.

The Land of Storybooks

At evening when the lamp is lit,
Around the fire my parents sit;
They sit at home and talk and sing,
And do not play at anything.

Now, with my little gun, I crawl
All in the dark along the wall,
And follow round the forest track
Away behind the sofa back.

There, in the night, where none can
    spy,
All in my hunter's camp I lie,
And play at books that I have read
Till it is time to go to bed.

These are the hills, these are the
    woods,
These are my starry solitudes;
And there the river by whose brink
The roaring lion comes to drink.

I see the others far away
As if in firelit camp they lay,
And I, like to an Indian scout,
Around their party prowled about.

So when my nurse comes in for me,
Home I return across the sea,
And go to bed with backward looks
At my dear land of Storybooks.

    —*Robert Louis Stevenson.*

Foreign Children

Little Indian, Sioux or Crow,
Little frosty Eskimo,
Little Turk or Japanee,
O! don't you wish that you were me?

You have seen the scarlet trees
And the lions over seas;
You have eaten ostrich eggs,
And turned the turtles off their legs.

You have curious things to eat,
I am fed on proper meat;
You must dwell beyond the foam,
But I am safe and live at home.

Little Indian, Sioux or Crow,
Little frosty Eskimo,
Little Turk or Japanee,
O! don't you wish that you were me?

—Robert Louis Stevenson.

The Wind

I saw you toss the kites on high
And blow the birds about the sky;
And all around I heard you pass,
Like ladies' skirts across the grass—
    O wind, a-blowing all day long,
    O wind, that sings so loud a song!

I saw the different things you did,
But always you yourself you hid.
I felt you push, I heard you call,
I could not see yourself at all—
    O wind, a-blowing all day long,
    O wind, that sings so loud a song!

O you that are so strong and cold,
O blower, are you young or old?
Are you a beast of field and tree,
Or just a stronger child than me?
    O wind, a-blowing all day long,
    O wind, that sings so loud a song!

                    —Robert Louis Stevenson.

The Lamplighter

My tea is nearly ready and the sun
    has left the sky;
It's time to take the window to see
    Leerie going by;
For every night at teatime and before
    you take your seat,
With lantern and with ladder he
    comes posting up the street.

Now Tom would be a driver and
    Maria go to sea,
And my papa's a banker and as rich
    as he can be;
But I, when I am stronger and can
    choose what I'm to do,
O Leerie, I'll go round at night and
    light the lamps with you!

For we are very lucky, with a lamp
    before the door,
And Leerie stops to light it as he
    lights so many more,
And Oh! before you hurry by with
    ladder and with light,
O Leerie, see a little child and nod
    to him to-night!

                —*Robert Louis Stevenson.*

From a Railway Carriage

Faster than fairies, faster than witches,
Bridges and houses, hedges and ditches;
And charging along like troops in a battle,
All through the meadows, the horses and cattle.

All the sights of the hill and the plain
Fly as thick as driving rain;
And ever again, in the wink of an eye,
Painted stations whistle by.

Here is a child who clambers and scrambles,
All by himself and gathering brambles;
Here is a tramp who stands and gazes,
And there is the green for stringing the daisies!

Here is a cart run away in the road,
Lumping along with man and load;
And here is a mill and there is a river:
Each a glimpse and gone forever!

—*Robert Louis Stevenson.*

The Ugly Duckling

It was glorious out in the country. Cornfields were waving, oats were green, and hay stood in great stacks in the meadows. Beyond the fields and meadows were great forests and pools of water. On a sunny slope stood a pleasant old farmhouse, and near it flowed a little stream of water. At the water's edge grew great burdocks, so high that little children could stand under them. The spot was as wild as the middle of a deep woods.

In this snug place sat a duck upon her nest watching for her young brood to hatch. At last one eggshell after another cracked open. And from each egg a little duckling stuck out its head and cried, "Peep, peep!"

"Quack! quack!" said the mother, and out they came as fast as they could. Then the mother let them look about as much as they liked, for green is good for the eyes.

"How big the world is!" said the little ducklings.

"Do you think this is all the world?" asked the mother. "Wait till you get to the garden. The big world extends far beyond it. Are you all out of your shells? No, the largest egg is still unbroken." So she sat down again.

"Well, how goes it?" asked an old duck who came to pay her a visit.

"There is one egg that will not hatch," said the duck, "but only look at the other ducklings. They look just like their father."

"Let me see the egg that will not hatch," said the visitor. "It must be a turkey's egg. The little turkey will not go into the water, and it will give you trouble. Take my advice and leave it."

"I think I will sit on it a little longer," said the mother duck. "A few days will not matter much."

At last the great egg cracked. "Peep! peep!" said the duckling, and out it tumbled. Oh, how large and ugly it was!

"Can it really be a turkey chick?" said

the mother. "We shall see when we get to the water."

Next day the mother duck went down to the water with all her little ones. She jumped into the water with a splash. "Quack! quack!" she cried, and one duckling after another plunged in. The water closed over their heads, but they all came up again. They swam about very prettily and the ugly gray duckling swam with them.

"No, he is not a turkey," said the mother. "Look how well he can use his legs. He is my own child, and he's not so very ugly."

"Quack! quack! Come with me now," said the mother. "I will lead you out into the great world and introduce you to the farmyard. But keep close to me, so that no one can step on you."

"Bow your heads before that old duck yonder, she is the grandest duck here. See, she has a red rag around her leg. That is a great honor. Come, now, don't turn your toes in. A well-bred duck turns its toes out, just like father and mother. Now bend your necks and say, Quack!"

They did as they were told, but the other ducks said, "Look, here comes another brood, and how ugly that one is! We don't want him here." Then one of the ducks, flew at the ugly duckling and bit him in the neck.

"Let him alone," said the mother; "he is doing no harm."

"But he is so ugly," said the duck who had bitten him. "He must be turned out."

"Those are pretty children that the mother has there," said the old duck with the rag around her leg. "They are all pretty but that one. He has not turned out well."

"He is not pretty, but he is a good child," said his mother, "and he swims as well as the others. I may even say he swims better. I think he will grow up to be pretty. He stayed too long in the egg." And she stroked his neck and smoothed his feathers.

When the turkey cock saw the duckling he blew himself up like a ship in full sail, and gobbled and grew quite red. The poor little duckling did not know what to do. The ducks bit him, and the hens pecked him.

The duckling was very unhappy and at last ran away. He flew over the hedge, and frightened the little birds in the bushes.

"They are afraid of me because I am so ugly," thought the duckling. Then he flew on farther and came to a moor where some wild ducks lived.

"What sort of duck are you?" they asked, coming around him.

The little duckling turned in every

direction and bowed as well as he knew how.

"You are really very ugly," said the wild ducks, and they swam away.

Poor duckling, how lonely he was! He lay among the reeds and drank some of the water of the moor.

At last there came two wild geese who had not been long out of the egg. That is why they were so saucy.

"Listen, friend," said one of them, "you are so ugly that I like you. Will you come with me and be a bird of passage? Not far from here is another moor, in which there are some pretty wild geese. It is a chance for you to get a wife, ugly as you are."

Bang! bang! and the geese fell dead in the swamp. Bang! bang! and whole flocks of wild geese rose up from the reeds. A great hunt was going on. The hunters lay hidden all around. Some were even sitting on the branches of the trees. The hunting dogs came splash! splash! into the swamp, and the rushes and reeds bent down on every side.

That was a fright for the poor duckling. He turned his head and put it under his wing. At that moment a great dog dashed close to him. His tongue hung far out of his mouth and his eyes glared at the duckling. He thrust out his nose, showed his sharp teeth, and, splash! splash! on he went without touching him.

"Well, let me be thankful," sighed the duckling; "I'm so ugly that even the dogs will not bite me." So he lay quite still while gun after gun was fired, and the shots rattled through the reeds.

Late in the day all became quiet, but even then the poor little thing dared not stir. He waited for several hours before he looked around, and then he ran over field and meadow as fast as he could.

Toward night he reached a poor little cottage. The hut was so old that it did not know on which side it should fall. That is why it remained standing at this time.

The door was open, for it had lost one of its hinges. The storm grew worse and worse. The poor duckling was too tired to go on, so he slipped through the open door into the room.

Here lived an old woman with her cat and her hen. The cat could arch his back and purr and give out sparks when his fur was stroked the wrong way. The hen had little short legs and was called "chick-a-biddy-short-shanks." She laid good eggs and the woman loved her as her own child.

In the morning the old woman found the strange duckling. She could not see very well and she thought he was a fat duck. "Now we shall have duck's eggs," said she. So the duckling was allowed to stay. He stayed three weeks but no eggs came.

Now, the cat thought he was the master of the house, and the hen thought she was the mistress, and they always said, "We are the world."

"Can you lay eggs?" asked the hen.

"No," said the duckling.

"Then you'll have the goodness to hold your tongue!"

And the cat said, "Can you curve your back and purr and give out sparks?"

"No," said the duckling.

"Then keep still when we are speaking."

So the duckling sat alone in the corner and was very unhappy. The fresh air and the sunshine came in at the open door, and he longed to be out on the water.

"What are you thinking of?" said the hen.

"It is so fine to swim on the water when the water closes over your head and you plunge to the bottom," said the duckling.

"Well, that is a queer sort of pleasure," said the hen; "I think you must be crazy. Ask the cat about it. He is the wisest animal I know. Ask him if he likes to swim on the water, or plunge to the bottom. Ask our mistress, the old woman. There is no one

in the world wiser than she. Do you think she has any wish to swim, or to let the water close over her head?"

"You do not understand me," said the duckling.

"What! we do not understand you? Then pray, who is to understand you? Do you think yourself wiser than the cat or the old woman? I won't say anything of myself. Be thankful for all we have done for you. Learn to lay eggs or to purr and give out sparks," said the hen.

"I think I will go out into the wide world," said the duckling.

"Yes, do go," said the hen.

And he went away. He swam on the water and dived, but he was lonesome, for all the animals passed him by because he was so ugly.

Now the autumn came and it was very cold. The air was heavy with hail and snowflakes, and on the fence stood a raven crying, "Croak! croak!" because he was so cold.

One evening a whole flock of great white birds came out of the bushes. They were swans. They had long slender necks and they uttered a strange cry.

As he watched them the ugly duckling felt quite strange and gave such a strange cry that it frightened even himself. He could not forget those beautiful, happy birds, and he loved them more than he had ever loved anyone.

The swans spread their wings and flew higher and higher. He watched them till they were out of sight. Then he dived to the bottom of the water.

The winter grew cold and the duckling swam around in the water to keep from freezing. Every night the hole in which he swam grew smaller and smaller. Then it froze so hard that the duckling had to use his legs to keep from freezing fast. At last he became tired and lay quite stiff and cold on the ice.

The next morning a farmer found the duckling and carried him home to his wife. The warm room soon revived him, but the children frightened him. In his terror he fluttered into the milk pan and splashed the milk about the room. The woman slapped her hands and that frightened him still more. He flew into the butter tub and then into the meal barrel. How strange he looked then! The children chased him with the fire tongs. They screamed and laughed at him. The door was open and he slipped out into the snow. All winter long he was cold and hungry.

Then the warm sun began to shine and

the duckling shook his wings and found they were strong. Soon he found himself in a beautiful garden. The willow trees bent their long green branches into the stream and the apple trees were in full bloom. And out of the thicket came the same beautiful white swans, swimming lightly over the smooth water.

"I will fly to those royal birds," he said. "They will kill me because I am so ugly, but it does not matter. It is better to be killed than to be bitten by the ducks, pecked by the hens, and beaten by everyone."

So he flew into the water and swam toward the beautiful birds. They saw him and swam to meet him.

The poor duckling bowed his head upon the water and said, "Only kill me." But the swans stroked his neck with their beaks.

Then in the clear water beneath him he saw another swan more beautiful than the others. "That is my image," he cried, "I am no longer an ugly duckling. I am a beautiful swan." And he hid his head under

his wing, for he was so happy he did not know what to do.

Some children came into the garden and cried, "See, a new swan has come and he is more beautiful than any of the others."

Then the young swan lifted his slender neck and, in the joy of his heart, said, "I never dreamed of such happiness when I was an ugly duckling."

—*Hans Christian Andersen.*

Thanksgiving Day

Over the river and through the wood,
    To grandfather's house we go;
        The horse knows the way
        To carry the sleigh
    Through the white and drifted snow.

Over the river and through the wood—
    Oh, how the wind does blow!
        It stings the toes
        And bites the nose,
    As over the ground we go.

Over the river and through the wood,
    To have a first-rate play.
        Hear the bells ring,
        "Ting-a-ling-ding!"
    Hurrah for Thanksgiving Day!

Over the river and through the wood,
    Trot fast, my dapple-gray!
        Spring over the ground,
        Like a hunting-hound!
For this is Thanksgiving Day.

Over the river and through the wood,
    And straight through the barn-yard gate.
        We seem to go
        Extremely slow,
It is so hard to wait!

Over the river and through the wood—
    Now grandmother's cap I spy!
        Hurrah for the fun!
        Is the pudding done?
Hurrah for pumpkin-pie!

                —*Lydia Maria Child.*

Who Stole the Bird's Nest?

"To-whit! to-whit! to-whee!
Will you listen to me?
Who stole four eggs I laid,
And the nice nest I made?"

"Not I," said the cow, "Moo-oo!
Such a thing I'd never do.
I gave you a wisp of hay,
But didn't take your nest away.
Not I," said the cow, "Moo-oo!
Such a thing I'd never do."

"To-whit! to-whit! to-whee!
Will you listen to me?
Who stole four eggs I laid,
And the nice nest I made?"

"Bob-o'-link! Bob-o'-link!
Now what do you think?
Who stole a nest away
From the plum-tree, to-day?"

"Not I," said the dog, "Bow-wow!
I wouldn't be so mean, I vow!
I gave hairs the nest to make,
But the nest I did not take.
Not I," said the dog, "Bow-wow!
I'm not so mean, anyhow."

"To-whit! to-whit! to-whee!
Will you listen to me?
Who stole four eggs I laid,
And the nice nest I made?"

"Bob-o'-link! Bob-o'-link!
Now what do you think?
Who stole a nest away
From the plum-tree, to-day?"

"Coo-coo! Coo-coo! Coo-coo!
Let me speak a word, too!
Who stole that pretty nest
From little yellow-breast?"

"Not I," said the sheep, "Oh, no!
I wouldn't treat a poor bird so.

I gave wool the nest to line,
But the nest was none of mine.
Baa! Baa!" said the sheep, "Oh, no!
I wouldn't treat a poor bird so."

"To-whit! to-whit! to-whee!
Will you listen to me?
Who stole four eggs I laid,
And the nice nest I made?"

"Bob-o'-link! Bob-o'-link
Now what do you think?
Who stole a nest away
From the plum-tree, to-day?"

"Coo-coo! Coo-coo! Coo-coo!
Let me speak a word, too!
Who stole that pretty nest
From little yellow-breast?"

"Caw! Caw!" cried the crow;
"I should like to know
What thief took away
A bird's nest to-day?"

"Cluck! Cluck!" said the hen;
"Don't ask me again,
  Why I haven't a chick
  Would do such a trick.
  We all gave her a feather,
  And she wove them together.
  I'd scorn to intrude
  On her and her brood.
  Cluck! Cluck!" said the hen,
"Don't ask me again."

"Chirr-a-whirr! Chirr-a-whirr!
  All the birds make a stir!
  Let us find out his name,
  And all cry 'For shame!'"

  A little boy hung down his head,
  And went and hid behind the bed,
  For he stole that pretty nest
  From poor little yellow-breast.
  And he felt so full of shame,
  He didn't like to tell his name.

—*Lydia Maria Child.*

The Bear and the Fox

It was in the spring. The trees were clothed in green and the earth was covered with flowers. It was then that the lion, the king of beasts, called his court together.

Soon all the beasts, both great and small, came in great numbers. Only Reynard the fox was absent. He knew that he was guilty of many misdeeds against the other beasts. He knew that if he came to court he put his life in danger.

The king heard the complaints of the wolf, the hound, and the cock against the fox. He decided that Reynard should appear before the court to answer the complaints. Then he said to Bruin the bear, "You shall take this message to Reynard. But remember, Bruin, that Reynard knows how to flatter even the wisest."

"Let me alone with Reynard," said Bruin; "if he mocks me I shall pay him back."

So the next morning Bruin set out. When he came to Reynard's castle the gate was shut. He knocked and knocked.

Then he shouted, "Sir Reynard, are you at home? I am Bruin, your kinsman, with a message from the king. You are summoned to appear at court to answer for your misdeeds. The king has taken a vow that if you fail to appear it shall cost you your life. So take the advice of a friend and come with me."

Reynard was lying near the gate basking in the sun. He lay quiet and listened to the bear. He made sure that Bruin was alone. Then he went into one of his holes. There he thought out what to do to disgrace Bruin and escape going to court.

At last he came forth and said, "Dear Uncle Bruin, how tired you must be. Come in and rest. The king should not have sent you on this long journey; you who are next to him in royal blood and riches. I am going to court to-morrow. I was not well enough to go to-day. I have been eating such strange new meat and it has made me ill."

"What is this strange meat?" asked Bruin.

"Uncle," replied the fox, "why do you care to know? It was only honeycomb. It was simple and mean. I was hungry and I ate too much."

"Do you call honeycomb simple and mean?" cried Bruin. "Come, my dear Reynard, and help me to some of this honey, and I will be your friend as long as I live."

"You are jesting with me," said Reynard.

"I am in earnest," cried Bruin. "For one lick of that honeycomb I will be your friend forever and I will stop the mouths of your enemies."

"If that is true, I can serve you," said the fox. "At the foot of this mountain lives a farmer, who has more honey than you could eat in seven years. I will take you to it."

The bear gave him many thanks and away they went. At last they came to an oak tree in which the farmer had driven a wedge.

"Dear Uncle," said Reynard, "in this tree there is more honey than you can eat. Put your nose inside this gap and you will find it. Do not eat too much. It might do you harm."

"Do not fear for me," said the bear.

Then he put his front paws into the gap and thrust his head in up to his ears.

When the fox saw this he ran and pulled the wedge out and left Bruin locked in the tree. The bear began to howl and to scratch with his hind feet. He made such a noise that the farmer heard it and ran out to see what was the matter.

And the fox from afar off cried, "Is

the honey good, Uncle? Do not eat too much."

When the farmer saw the bear he called to his neighbors to come and see. Men, women, and children came running out, some with one weapon and some with another.

Poor Bruin, hearing all this noise, pulled and pulled till he had pulled himself free; but he left his ears behind and the skin of his forepaws. Then he made a leap to get away and fell into the river.

Meanwhile the fox was feeling gay. "All is well," he said, "my enemy is dead and I shall not have to go to court." So he stole a fat hen and started home. When he came to the river he saw the bear resting on the bank. He was filled with fear, but he said, "Well, Uncle, did you eat all the honey? It has made you sick. Where are your ears and your gloves?"

Filled with rage, the bear crept to the water. He plunged in and swam down the stream. When he came to a flat bank he landed and lay there, sick and sore. Then he said to himself, "How can I get back to court? I cannot walk, yet to the court I must go, for Reynard shall pay for this."

So he set his tail on the ground and tumbled his body over and over. After many days he tumbled into court.

"Who can this strange creature be?" they all cried.

But when the king saw him he said, "It is Bruin; who could have wounded him like this?"

"O king," said Bruin, "it was that false Reynard who has brought me to disgrace."

"How dare he do this?" said the king. "I swear now that I shall make him tremble." Whereupon the king sent for his council.

It was decided that Reynard should again be summoned to court. He must be made to answer for all his wrong doing. So Tibert the cat was chosen to get Reynard, for the cat was known for his great wisdom.

—*Reynard the Fox*.

The Fox and the Wolf

Once a wolf came to Reynard the fox in the woods and said he was hungry. The fox said he was hungry too, so off they set in search of food.

They traveled half a day without finding anything. At last, on the side of a hill, they saw a hole covered with branches and heard a low growling within. "There must be game in there," said the fox. "Go inside and see what you can find."

The wolf began to whine and said, "I am

weak from hunger, I will stay here under the trees and wait. You go in to see if you can find anything. You have so much more wit and cunning to meet strangers than I have."

So the fox entered the hole, and there sat an ape. Her wide mouth was filled with great ugly teeth, and her fiery eyes stared savagely at him. By her side lay her brood of young ones, as fierce as she. As the fox drew near they all gaped wide their mouths and stared at him. Seeing no way of escape, he made bold and said, "Long life and happiness to you, my dear aunt. Let me wish you joy with your children. They are the fairest I have ever seen. You may well be proud of them."

"My dear Reynard," replied the ape, "you are welcome. For the rest of my life I shall thank you for this visit. You are known everywhere for your wit and judgment, and I beg you to take charge of my children and teach them how to live in the world.

The fox answered, "My dear aunt, what I can do for you day or night shall be done.

I am at your command." He then turned to go.

"My dear friend," said the ape, "you must not leave till you have eaten something." Then she led the way to her great store of food. When he had eaten all he wanted, she said, "Come often to see me, dear Reynard."

When the fox came out of the cave, the wolf was waiting under the tree. "What did you find in the hole there?" he asked.

"Creep into the hole, Uncle," said the fox. "There you will find an ape with her brood. If you please them with fair words, they will treat you with kindness and give you plenty of food."

So the wolf went in. There sat the apes in all their filth and dirt. No sooner had he seen them than he cried out, "What ugly beasts are these? Are all these creatures your children? Go drown them! They are so ugly that they will scare all the world."

"They are my children and I am their

mother," said the ape. "If they displease you, go away."

The wolf answered, "First I would eat of your meat."

"I have no meat for you," she replied, looking savagely at him.

"You have," he snarled. "Give it to me or I shall help myself. You have enough here for ten."

The ape and all her children started at him and bit him and scratched him with their teeth and nails. He howled and yelped and ran out of the cave as fast as he could.

As he came out he said, "I wish I had them outside and I would make them pay for this."

"I fear you have not made good use of your tongue," said the fox.

"I spoke what I thought," said the wolf.

"And you have received your reward," said the fox.

—Reynard the Fox.

The Man and the Serpent

Once a serpent, who was going through a hedge, was caught in a snare. The more he struggled, the tighter he drew the cord about his neck. There was no way of escape. He cried out to a man who was passing by, "Help me or I shall perish."

The man took pity on him and said, "I

will release you if you will promise to do me no harm." The serpent made a solemn promise not to harm him at that time or any time thereafter. So the man loosed the noose and set the serpent free.

The serpent kept his promise for a time, but one day he became very hungry and struck at the man to kill him. The man started back and cried, "Have you forgotten your promise? Did you not promise to do me no harm?"

Whereupon the serpent answered, "I am hungry and my hunger compels me to kill you. Hunger knows no law."

"Well, at least," said the man, "let me live until we meet someone who will judge fairly between us."

The serpent agreed and they went on together till they met a raven and his son. The serpent told them of his hunger and the raven, hoping to get his share, said, "Yes, hunger frees the serpent from his oath."

But the man said, "Shall a person who

lives by robbing be a judge, and shall there be but one judge? Let us submit this matter to three or four and hear them all."

The serpent agreed to this and they went on till they met a wolf and a bear. And the bear and the wolf both said, "Yes, hunger knows no law." Then with a terrible hissing the serpent darted at the man.

But the man leaped aside and said, "Would you kill the friend who saved your life?"

The serpent replied, "Twice have the judges spoken and twice was the judgment against you."

The man replied, "They are thieves themselves. Let us go to your king, whom you all trust. What he says I will abide by."

Then the man, the serpent, the bear, the wolf and the ravens came to the court of the king and told their story. The king was greatly troubled. He said, "It is hard to condemn the man, for he has been kind;

but still I have pity for the serpent. He must have food to save his life."

So the king called his court together, but no one was able to judge the case. Then he asked Reynard the fox to give his judgment. Reynard heard both sides. Then he said, "First let me see the serpent in the noose just as the man found him." So they all went to the hedge, and the serpent was again tied in the noose.

Then the king said, "Now, Reynard, what judgment will you give?"

Reynard replied, "O, King, they are now in the same place they were before the promise was given. Let the man loose the serpent if it now please him, knowing that hunger releases the serpent from his promise."

The king honored Reynard's judgment, and said, "Your wisdom has saved the honor of the court."

—Reynard the Fox.

The Fox as Herdsman

Once on a time there was a woman who went out to hire a herdsman, and she met a bear.

"Whither away, Goody?" said Bruin.

"Oh, I'm going out to hire a herdsman," answered the woman.

"Why not have me for a herdsman?" said Bruin.

"Well, why not," said the woman, "if you only know how to call the flock? Just let me hear you call."

"Ow, Ow!" growled the bear.

"No, no! I won't have you," said the woman as soon as she heard him say that, and off she went on her way.

When she had gone a bit farther she met a wolf.

"Whither away, Goody?" said the wolf.

"Oh," said she, "I'm going out to hire a herdsman."

"Why not have me for a herdsman?" said the wolf.

"Well, why not, if you can only call the flock? Let me hear you call," said she.

"Uh, Uh!" said the wolf.

"No, no!" said the woman, "you'll never do for me."

Well, after she had gone a while longer she met a fox.

"Whither away, Goody?" asked the fox.

"Oh, I'm just going out to hire a herdsman," said the woman.

"Why not have me for a herdsman?" asked the fox.

"Well, why not," said she, "if you only know how to call the flock? Let me hear you call."

"Dil-dal-holom!" sang out the fox in a fine clear voice.

"Yes, I'll have you for my herdsman," said the woman, and she set the fox to herd her flock.

The first day the fox was herdsman he ate up all the woman's goats; the next day he made an end of all her sheep; and the third day he ate up all her cows. So, when he came home at even, the woman asked what he had done with all her flocks.

"Oh!" said the fox, "their skulls are in the stream, and their bodies in the holt."

Now, the Goody stood and churned when the fox said this, but she thought she might as well step out and see after her flock. While she was away the fox crept into the churn and ate up the cream. When Goody came back and saw that she fell into a rage. She snatched up the little morsel of cream that was left and threw it at the fox as he ran off. He got a dab of it on the end of his tail, and that's the reason why the fox has a white tip to his brush.

—Norse Folk Tale.

The Brown Thrush

There's a merry brown thrush sitting
    up in the tree,
He's singing to me! He's singing to me!
And what does he say, little girl, little boy?
"Oh, the world's running over with joy!

  Don't you hear? don't you see?
  Hush! look! in my tree,
I'm as happy as happy can be!"

And the brown thrush keeps singing, "A
   nest do you see,
And five eggs hid by me in the juniper tree?
Don't meddle! don't touch! little girl, little
   boy,
Or the world will lose some of its joy!
  Now I'm glad! now I'm free!
  And I always shall be,
If you never bring sorrow to me."

So the merry brown thrush sings away in
   the tree,
To you and to me, to you and to me.
And he sings all the day, little girl, little boy,
"Oh, the world's running over with joy!"
  But long it won't be,
  Don't you know? don't you see?
Unless we are as good as can be.

—Lucy Larcom.

Berrying Song

Ho! for the hills in summer!
   Ho! for the rocky shade,
Where the ground pine trails neath the
      fern-leaves,
   Deep in the mossy glade.

Up in the dewy sunrise,
   Waked by the robin's trill;
Up and away, a-berrying,
   To the pastures on the hill!

Red lilies blaze out of the thicket;
   Wild roses blush here and there:
There's a sweetness in all the breezes,
   There's health in each breath of air.

We'll garland our baskets with blossoms,
   And sit on the rocks and sing,
And tell one another old stories,
   Till the trees long shadows fling.

Then homeward with laughter and carol,
   Mocking the echoes shrill,
O, merry it is a-berrying
   In the pastures on the hill!

                —*Lucy Larcom.*

Little Nannie

Light-footed Nannie,
   Where have you been?
"Chasing the sunbeams
   Into the glen;
Plunging through silver lakes
   After the moon;
Tracking o'er meadows
   The footsteps of June."

Sunny-eyed Nannie,
   What did you see?
"Saw the fays sewing
   Green leaves on a tree;
Saw the waves counting
   The eyes of the stars;
Saw cloud-lambs sleeping
   By sunset's red bars."

Listening Nannie,
   What did you hear?
"Heard the rain asking
   A rose to appear;
Heard the woods tell
   When the wind whistled wrong;

Heard the stream flow
   Where the bird drinks his song."

Nannie, dear Nannie,
   Oh, take me with you,
To run and to listen,
   And see as you do.
"Nay, nay! you must borrow
   My ear and my eye,
Or the beauty will vanish,
   The music will die."

—Lucy Larcom.

Calling the Violet

Dear little Violet,
    Don't be afraid!
Lift your blue eyes
    From the rock's mossy shade!
All the birds call for you
    Out of the sky:
May is here waiting,
    And here, too, am I.

Why do you shiver so,
    Violet sweet?
Soft is the meadow grass
    Under your feet.
Wrapped in your hood of green,
    Violet, why
Peep from your earth-door
    So silent and shy?

Trickle the little brooks
    Close to your bed;
Softest of fleecy clouds
    Float overhead;
"Ready and waiting!"
    The slender reeds sigh:
"Ready and waiting!"
    We sing—May and I.

Come, pretty Violet,
    Winter's away;
Come, for without you
    May isn't May.

Down through the sunshine
   Wings flutter and fly;—
Quick, little Violet,
   Open your eye!

Hear the rain whisper,
   "Dear Violet, Come!"
How can you stay
   In your underground home?
Up in the pine-boughs
   For you the winds sigh,
Homesick to see you,
   Are we—May and I.

Ha! though you care not
   For call or for shout;
Yon troop of sunbeams
   Are winning you out.
Now all is beautiful
   Under the sky;
May's here,—and Violets!
   Winter, good-by!

—Lucy Larcom.

If I Were a Sunbeam

"If I were a sunbeam,
 I know what I'd do:
 I would seek white lilies
 Rainy woodlands through;
 I would steal among them,
 Softest light I'd shed,
 Until every lily
 Raised its drooping head.

"If I were a sunbeam,
 I know where I'd go:
 Into lowliest hovels
 Dark with want and woe."

 Art thou not a sunbeam,
 Child whose life is glad
 With an inner radiance
 Sunshine never had?
 Oh, as God has blessed thee,
 Scatter rays divine!
 For there is no sunbeam
 But must die, or shine.

—Lucy Larcom.

Alice in Wonderland

Alice was tired of sitting on the bank. She had peeped into the book her sister was reading, but it had no pictures in it. "What is the use of a book without pictures in it?" thought Alice.

It was a hot day and she was sleepy. Suddenly a white rabbit with pink eyes ran close to her. Alice heard him say, "Oh dear! Oh dear! I shall be late!" And he took a watch out of his pocket, looked at it, and then hurried on. Alice had never before seen a rabbit with a watch. She ran across the field after it, and was just in time to see it pop down a large rabbit hole under the hedge.

In another moment in went Alice after it, and she found herself falling down a very steep well.

Either the well was very deep or she fell very slowly, for she had plenty of time as she went down to look about her.

Down, down, down. Would the fall never come to an end? "I wonder how many miles I've fallen by this time?" she said aloud. "I must be getting near the center of the earth. I wonder if I shall fall right through the earth! How funny it will seem to come out among the people who walk with their heads downwards!"

Suddenly, thump! thump! and Alice came down upon a heap of sticks and dry leaves, and the fall was over. She was not a bit hurt and jumped to her feet in a moment. She looked up, but it was dark overhead. Before her was another long passage, and the White Rabbit was still in sight, hurrying down it. There was not a moment to be lost. Away went Alice like the wind, and she was just in time to hear the rabbit say as it turned the corner, "Oh, my ears and whiskers, how late it's getting!"

Alice was close behind it when she turned the corner, but the rabbit was nowhere to be seen. She found herself in a long hall, which was lighted up by a row of lamps hanging from the roof.

There were doors all round the hall, but they were locked. Alice went down one side and up the other. Then she walked down the middle, wondering how she was ever to get out again.

Suddenly she came upon a little three-legged table of solid glass. There was nothing on it but a tiny golden key. Alice first thought that this might belong to one of the doors of the hall; but alas! either the locks were too large or the key was too small, for it would not open any of them. On the second time round, she came upon a curtain she had not seen before, and behind it was a little door about fifteen inches high. She tried the golden key in the lock, and it fitted.

Alice opened the door and found that it led into a small passage, not much larger than a rat hole. She knelt down and looked along the passage into the loveliest garden you ever saw. How she longed to get out of that dark hall and wander about among those bright flowers and those cool fountains. But she could not even get her head through the doorway.

"And even if my head would go through," thought Alice, "it would be of very little use without my shoulders. Oh, how I wish I could shut up like a telescope. I think I could, if I only knew how to begin."

There seemed to be no use in waiting by the little door, so she went back to the table. She hoped she might find another key on it, or a book of rules for shutting people up, like telescopes. This time she found a little bottle on it, and tied round the neck of it was a paper label, with the words "Drink Me," printed on it in large letters.

"I'll look first," she said, "and see whether it's marked 'poison' or not."

It was not marked "poison," so Alice tasted it, and finding it a nice flavor of cherry tart, custard, pine-apple, roast turkey, candy, and hot buttered toast, she very soon finished it.

"What a curious feeling!" said Alice. "I must be shutting up like a telescope!"

And so she was indeed. She was now only ten inches high, and her face brightened up at the thought that she was now the right size for going through the door into that lovely garden. She waited for a few minutes to see if she were going to shrink any more. She felt a little nervous about this, "For it might end, you know, in my going out like a candle," said she. "I wonder what I should be like then?"

Alice tried to fancy what the flame of a candle looks like after the candle is blown out, for she could not remember ever having seen such a thing.

After a while, finding that nothing more happened, she decided to go into the garden. But, alas for poor Alice! when she got to the door she found she had forgotten the little golden key. When she went back to the table for it she could not reach it. She tried to climb up one of the legs of the table, but it was too slippery.

Soon her eye fell on a little glass box that was lying under the table. She opened it and found in it a very small cake, on which the words "Eat Me" were marked in currants.

"Well, I'll eat it," said Alice, "and if it makes me grow larger, I can reach the key. If it makes me grow smaller, I can creep under the door. So either way I'll get into the garden, and I don't care which happens!"

She ate a little bit and said to herself, "Which way? Which way?"

She held her hand on the top of her head to feel which way she was growing:

"Curiouser and Curiouser!" cried Alice. She was so much surprised that for a moment she forgot how to speak good English. "Now I'm opening out like the largest telescope that ever was! Good-bye, feet!" For when she looked down at her feet they seemed to be almost out of sight, they were getting so far away. "Oh, my poor little feet; I wonder who will put on your shoes and stockings for you now, dears? I'm sure I shan't be able! I shall be a great deal too far off to trouble myself about you. You must manage the best way you can. But I must be kind to them," thought Alice, "or perhaps they won't walk the way I want to go! Let me see; I'll give them a new pair of boots for Christmas. How funny it will seem, sending presents to my feet! How odd the directions will look!

> **Alice's Right Foot, Esq.,**
>   **Hearthrug,**
>   **near the Fender,**
>   **(With Alice's love).**

Oh dear, what nonsense I'm talking!"

Just at this moment her head struck against the roof of the hall. In fact she was now more than nine feet high, and she at once took up the little golden key and hurried off to the garden door.

Poor Alice! To get through was more hopeless than ever, so she sat down and began to cry again.

"You ought to be ashamed of yourself," said Alice; "a great girl like you, to go on crying in this way! Stop this moment, I tell you!" But she went on all the same, shedding gallons of tears, until there was a large pool all around her, about four inches deep.

After a time she heard a little patter of feet in the distance and she dried her eyes to see what was coming. It was the White Rabbit, splendidly dressed, with a pair of

white kid gloves in one hand and a fan in the other. He came trotting along in a great hurry, muttering to himself as he came, "Oh! the Queen, the Queen! Oh! Won't she be savage if I have kept her waiting!" Alice felt so hopeless that she was ready to ask help of anyone. So, when the rabbit came near her, she began in a low, timid voice, "If you please, sir,—" The Rabbit dropped the white kid gloves and the fan, and skurried away into the darkness as hard as he could go.

Alice took up the fan and gloves. The hall was very hot and she kept on fanning herself all the time she went on talking. "Dear, dear! How queer everything is to-day! I wonder if I've been changed in the night? But if I am changed the next question is, Who in the World am I? And that's the great puzzle." And she began thinking over all the children she knew, to see if she could have changed into any of them.

Alice looked down at her hands and was surprised to find that she had put on one of the Rabbit's kid gloves. "How can I have done that?" she thought. "I must be growing small again." She got up and went to the table to measure herself by it, and found that she was now about two feet high, and was still shrinking. She soon found out that the cause of this was the fan she was holding. She dropped it hastily, just in time to save herself from shrinking away altogether.

"That was a narrow escape!" said Alice, glad to find herself still alive. "Now for the garden!" And she ran back to the little door, but the little door was shut and the little golden key was lying on the glass table as before. "Things are worse than ever," thought the poor child, "for I never was so small as this before." As she said this her foot slipped. Splash! she was up to her chin in salt water.

"I wish I had not cried so much!" said Alice, as she swam about, trying to find her way out. "I shall be punished for it now, I suppose, by being drowned in my own tears! That will be a queer thing, to be sure! However, everything is queer to-day."

She swam around for a little while. Then she swam to the shore. Poor Alice looked about her and began to cry, for she was very lonely.

After awhile she heard the patter of little feet. She looked, and there was the White Rabbit, trotting slowly back again and looking about as he went, as if he had lost something. She heard him muttering, "The Queen! the Queen! Oh, my dear paws! Oh, my fur and whiskers! Where can I have dropped them, I wonder?" Alice guessed in a moment that he was looking for the fan and the pair of white kid gloves, and she, too, began hunting about for them, but they were nowhere to be seen.

Soon the Rabbit noticed Alice and called out to her in an angry tone: "Why, Mary Ann, what are you doing here? Run home this moment and fetch me a pair of gloves and a fan! Quick!" Alice was so frightened that she ran off in the direction he pointed to, without trying to explain the mistake.

"He took me for his housemaid," she said to herself as she ran. "How surprised he will be when he finds out who I am! But I'd better take him his fan and gloves." As she said this, she came upon a neat little house. On the door was a bright brass plate with the name "W. Rabbit" upon it. She went in without knocking and went upstairs. She feared she should meet the real

Mary Ann, and be turned out of the house before she had found the fan and gloves. "How queer it seems," Alice said to herself, "to be going messages for a rabbit!"

Alice had found her way into a tidy little room with a table in the window, and on it was a fan and two or three pairs of tiny white kid gloves. She took up the fan and a pair of the gloves, and was just about to leave the room when her eyes fell upon a little bottle near the looking glass. There was no label this time with the words "Drink Me." However, she put it to her lips. "I know something strange is sure to happen," she said to herself, "whenever I eat or drink anything; so I'll just see what this bottle does. I do hope it will make me grow large again, for I'm quite tired of being so small."

It did so. Before she had drunk half the bottle she found her head pressing against the ceiling, and she had to stoop to save her neck from being broken. She put down the bottle, saying to herself, "That's quite enough. I hope I shan't grow any more. I do wish I hadn't drunk quite so much."

It was too late to wish that. She went on growing and growing, and very soon had to kneel on the floor. In another minute there was not even room for this, and she tried to lie down, with one elbow against the floor and the other arm curled round her head. Still she went on growing. At last she put one arm out of the window and one foot up the chimney and said to herself, "Now I can do no more, whatever happens. What will become of me?"

Luckily for Alice, the magic bottle had now had its full effect, and she grew no larger. Still it was very uncomfortable, and there seemed no chance of her getting out of the room again. No wonder she felt unhappy.

"It was much pleasanter at home," thought poor Alice. "I almost wish I hadn't gone down that rabbit hole. Yet this sort of life is curious. When I grow up I'll write a book about it. But I'm grown up now," she added; "at least there's no room to grow any more here."

"Mary Ann! Mary Ann!" said a voice outside, "bring my gloves this moment!" Then came a little pattering of feet on the stairs. Alice knew it was the Rabbit coming to look for her, and she trembled till she shook the house.

Presently, the Rabbit came up to the door and tried to open it, but Alice's elbow was pressed against it; she heard him say to himself, "Then I'll go round and get in at the window."

"That you won't!" thought Alice, and waiting till she heard the Rabbit just under the window, she suddenly spread out her hand and made a snatch in the air. She did not get hold of anything, but she heard a little shriek and a fall.

Next came the Rabbit's angry voice, "Pat! Pat! Where are you?"

And then came a voice she had never heard before, "Sure, then, I'm here, digging for apples, yer honor!"

"Digging for apples!" said the Rabbit. "Come and help me out of this! Now tell me, Pat, what's that in the window?"

"Sure, it's an arm, your honor!"

"An arm, you goose! Who ever saw one so big. Why, it fills the whole window!"

"Sure it does, yer honor; but it's an arm for all that."

"Well, it has no business there. Go and take it away!"

There was a long silence after this, and Alice could hear whispers, "Sure, I don't like it, yer honor, at all!"

"Do as I tell you!" said the Rabbit.

At last she spread out her hand again and made another snatch in the air. This time there were two little shrieks. "I wonder what they'll do next?" thought Alice.

She waited for some time, without hearing anything more. At last came a rumble of little cart wheels, and the sound of many voices. She made out the words: "Where's the other ladder?—Who's to go down the chimney? Bill's got to go down. Here, Bill!

the master says you've got to go down the chimney!"

"I wouldn't be in Bill's place for a good deal," thought Alice. "This fireplace is narrow, but I think I can kick a little."

She drew her foot as far down the chimney as she could, and waited till she heard a scratching in the chimney. Then she gave one sharp kick, and waited to see what would happen next.

The first thing she heard was, "There goes Bill! Catch him, you by the hedge!

Hold up his head—How was it, old fellow? What happened to you? Tell us about it."

Then a little voice said, "All I know is, something came to me like a Jack-in-the-box, and up I went like a skyrocket!"

There was a dead silence, and Alice thought to herself, "I wonder what they will do next! If they had any sense, they'd take the roof off." After a minute or two they began moving about again, and Alice heard the Rabbit say, "A barrowful will do."

"A barrowful of what?" thought Alice; but she had not long to wonder, for the next moment a shower of little pebbles came in at the window, and some of them hit her in the face. "I'll put a stop to this," she said to herself, and shouted out, "you'd better not do that again!"

Alice saw the pebbles turn into little cakes as they lay on the floor. A bright idea came into her head. "If I eat one of these cakes, it may make me smaller. It can't make me any larger," so she ate one of the cakes and began to shrink.

As soon as she was small enough to get through the door, she ran out of the house. She found a crowd of little animals and birds outside. The poor little lizard, Bill, was in the middle, being held up by two guinea-pigs who were giving it something out of a bottle. They all made a rush at Alice, but she ran off as hard as she could and soon found herself safe in the thick wood.

"The first thing I've got to do," said Alice to herself, as she wandered about in the Wood, "is to grow to my right size again; and the second thing is to find my way into that lovely garden."

Just as she said this, she noticed that one of the trees had a door leading right into it. "That's very curious!" she thought. "But everything is curious to-day. I think I may as well go in at once." And in she went.

Once more she found herself in the long hall and close to the little glass table. "Now,

I'll do better this time," she thought, and she took the little golden key, and unlocked the door that led into the garden. Then she nibbled the cake till she was about a foot high; and she walked down a little passage into the beautiful garden, among the bright flower-beds and the cool fountains.

Soon she heard her sister say, "Wake up, Alice dear. What a long sleep you have had."

—Arranged from Lewis Carroll's
"Alice in Wonderland."

Wynken, Blynken, and Nod

Wynken, Blynken, and Nod one night
  Sailed off in a wooden shoe—
Sailed on a river of crystal light,
  Into a sea of dew.
"Where are you going, and what do you
    wish?"
  The old moon asked the three.

"We have come to fish for the herring fish
  That live in this beautiful sea;

Nets of silver and gold have we!"
>Said Wynken,
>Blynken,
>And Nod.

The old moon laughed and sang a song,
>As they rocked in the wooden shoe,
And the wind that sped them all night
>long
>Ruffled the waves of dew.
The little stars were the herring fish
>That lived in that beautiful sea—
"Now cast your nets wherever you wish—
>Never afeard are we;"
So cried the stars to the fishermen three:
>Wynken,
>Blynken,
>And Nod.

All night long their nets they threw
>To the stars in the twinkling foam;
Then down from the skies came the
>wooden shoe,
>Bringing the fishermen home.
'Twas all so pretty a sail it seemed
>As if it could not be,

And some folks thought 'twas a dream
        they dreamed
Of sailing that beautiful sea—
But I shall name you the fishermen three:
        Wynken,
        Blynken,
        And Nod.

Wynken and Blynken are two little eyes,
    And Nod is a little head,
And the wooden shoe that sailed the skies
    Is a wee one's trundle-bed.
So shut your eyes while mother sings
    Of wonderful sights that be,
And you shall see the beautiful things
    As you rock in the misty sea,
Where the old shoe rocked the fishermen
        three:
        Wynken,
        Blynken,
        And Nod.

—Eugene Field.

The Shut-Eye Train

Come, my little one, with me!
There are wondrous sights to see
    As the evening shadows fall;
  In your pretty cap and gown,
    Don't detain
    The Shut-Eye train—
"Ting-a-ling!" the bell it goeth,
"Toot-toot!" the whistle bloweth,
And we hear the warning call:
"All aboard for Shut-Eye Town!"

Over hill and over plain
Soon will speed the Shut-Eye train!
    Through the blue where bloom the
        stars
    And the Mother Moon looks down
      We'll away
      To land of Fay—
    Oh, the sights that we shall see there!
    Come, my little one, with me there—
'Tis a goodly train of cars—
All aboard for Shut-Eye Town!

Swifter than a wild bird's flight,
Through the realms of fleecy light
    We shall speed and speed away!
    Let the Night in envy frown—
      What care we
      How wroth she be!
    To the Balow-land above us,
    To the Balow-folk who love us,
Let us hasten while we may—
All aboard for Shut-Eye Town!

Shut-Eye Town is passing fair—
Golden dreams await us there;
 We shall dream those dreams, my dear,
 Till the Mother Moon goes down—
  See unfold
   Delights untold!
 And in those mysterious places
 We shall see beloved faces
And beloved voices hear
In the grace of Shut-Eye Town!

Heavy are your eyes, my sweet,
Weary are your little feet—
 Nestle closer up to me
 In your pretty cap and gown;
  Don't detain
   The Shut-Eye train!
 "Ting-a-ling!" the bell it goeth,
 "Toot-toot!" the whistle bloweth
Oh, the sights that we shall see!
All aboard for Shut-Eye Town!

—Eugene Field.

The Duel

The gingham dog and the calico cat
Side by side on the table sat;
'Twas half-past twelve, and (what do you
         think!)
Nor one nor t'other had slept a wink!
    The old Dutch clock and the Chinese
          plate
    Appeared to know as sure as fate
There was going to be a terrible spat.
    (I wasn't there: I simply state
    What was told to me by the Chinese
          plate!)

The gingham dog went "Bow-wow-wow!"
And the calico cat replied "Mee-ow!"
The air was littered, an hour or so,
With bits of gingham and calico,
    While the old Dutch clock in the
          chimney-place
    Up with its hands before its face,
For it always dreaded a family row!
    (Now mind: I'm only telling you
    What the old Dutch clock declares is
          true!)

The Chinese plate looked very blue,
And wailed, "Oh, dear! what shall we do!"
But the gingham dog and the calico cat
Wallowed this way and tumbled that,
    Employing every tooth and claw
    In the awfullest way you ever saw—
And, oh! how the gingham and calico
        flew!
    (Don't fancy I exaggerate—
    I got my news from the Chinese
        plate!)

Next morning, where the two had sat,
They found no trace of dog or cat;
And some folks think unto this day
That burglars stole that pair away!
    But the truth about the cat and pup
    Is this: they ate each other up!
Now what do you really think of that
    (The old Dutch clock it told me so,
    And that is how I came to know.)

                      —*Eugene Field.*

The Snow-Image

One day after a great snowstorm, Violet and Peony asked to run out to play in the snow. The children's playground was a little garden in front of the house, with two or three plum trees, and some rose-bushes in it. The trees and shrubs were covered with snow and icicles.

"Yes, you may go out and play in the snow," said their mother, and she bundled them up in woolen jackets, put comforters round their necks, and mittens on their hands. Then she gave them each a kiss and out went the two children with a hop, skip and jump, into the very heart of a big snow-drift. Violet soon came out like a snow bunting, while Peony floundered out with his round face in full bloom.

"You look like a snow-image, Peony," said Violet, "if your cheeks were not so red. Let us make a snow-image—an image of a little girl, and she shall be our little sister. She shall run about and play with us all winter long. Won't it be nice?"

"Oh, yes!" cried Peony, as plainly as he could speak, for he was but a little boy. "That will be nice, and mamma shall see it."

"Yes," answered Violet, "mamma shall see the new little girl, but she must not make her come into the warm parlor, for our little snow-sister, will not love the warmth."

So the children began making a snow-image. They seemed to think they could make a live little girl out of the snow.

There was a busy hum of children's

voices as Violet and Peony worked together. Violet seemed to be the leader, while Peony brought her the snow from far and near.

"Peony, Peony!" cried Violet, for her brother was at the other side of the garden, "bring me those wreaths of snow on the lower branches of the pear tree. You can climb on the snowdrift, Peony, and reach them easily. I must have them to make ringlets for our snow-sister's head."

In a moment the little boy cried, "Here they are, Violet. Take care you do not break them. How pretty!"

"Does she not look sweet?" said Violet, "and now we must have some little shining bits of ice, to make her eyes bright. Mamma will see how very beautiful she is, but papa will say, 'Tush! nonsense! Come in out of the cold!'"

"Let us call mamma to look out," said Peony. Then he shouted, "Mamma! Mamma! Look out and see what a nice little girl we are making."

The mother put down her work, looked

out of the window, and saw the two children at work. "They do everything better than other children," said she, "no wonder they make pretty snow-images!"

"What a nice playmate she will be for us, all winter long!" said Violet. "I hope Papa will not be afraid she will give us a cold. Won't you love her dearly, Peony?"

"Yes," cried Peony, "and I will hug her, and she shall sit down close to me and drink some of my warm milk."

"Oh, no, Peony!" answered Violet, gravely, "that will not do at all. Warm milk will not be good for our little sister. Snow people eat nothing but icicles. No, no, Peony, we must not give her anything warm to drink."

There was a minute or two of silence; for Peony, whose short legs were never weary, had gone again to the other side of the garden. All of a sudden Violet cried out, "Look here, Peony! Come quickly! A light has been shining on her cheeks out of the rose colored cloud, and the color does not go away. Is not that beautiful?"

"Yes, it is beau-ti-ful," answered Peony. "O Violet, look at her hair; it is like gold."

"That color, you know, comes from the golden clouds we see up in the sky," said Violet. "She is almost finished now. But her lips must be made very red, redder than her cheeks. Perhaps, Peony, it will make them red if we both kiss them."

The mother heard two little smacks, as if both children were kissing the snow-image on its frozen mouth. This did not seem to make the lips quite red enough, so Violet proposed that the snow-child should kiss Peony's cheek.

"Come, little snow-sister, kiss me!" cried Peony.

"There she has kissed you," said Violet, "and now her lips are very red. She blushed a little, too."

"Oh, what a cold kiss!" cried Peony.

Just then the pure west wind came sweeping through the garden and rattled the parlor windows. It sounded so cold that the mother was about to call the two children in, when they both cried out to her with one voice:

"Mamma! Mamma! We have finished our little snow-sister, and she is running about the garden with us."

"Dear Mamma!" cried Violet, "look out and see what a sweet playmate we have."

The mother looked and there she saw a small white figure with rosy cheeks and golden ringlets, playing about the garden with the two children. Violet and Peony played with her, as if the three had been playmates all their lives. The mother thought it must be a neighbor's child who had run across the street to play with them. So she went to the door to invite the little runaway into her warm parlor.

As she looked she wondered if it was a real child after all, or only a wreath of snow blown hither and thither by the cold west wind, for there was something very strange about the child. Among all the children of the neighborhood the mother could remember no such lovely face with golden ringlets tossing about the forehead and cheeks. The child's white dress fluttered in the breeze, and her small feet had nothing on them but a pair of white slippers. Nevertheless she danced so lightly over the snow that the tips of her toes left no print on its surface. Violet could just keep pace with her, while Peony's short legs kept him behind.

Once the strange child placed herself between Violet and Peony and, taking a hand of each, skipped merrily forward. But

Peony pulled away his little fist and began to rub it as if his fingers were tingling with cold, and Violet drew away her hand, saying it was better not to take hold of hands.

The white figure said not a word, but danced about as merrily as before. If Violet and Peony would not play with her, she could find just as good a playmate in the cold west wind which kept blowing her all about the garden.

All this while the mother stood at the door, wondering how the little girl could look so much like a flying snowdrift, or a snowdrift could look so very like a little girl.

She called Violet and whispered to her, "Violet, my darling, what is this child's name? Does she live near us?"

"Why Mamma," answered Violet, "this is our little snow-sister whom we have just made!"

"Yes," cried Peony, "this is our snow-image! Is it not a nice little child?"

At this instant a flock of snowbirds came fluttering through the air. They

flew at once to the white-robed child and fluttered about her head. They seemed to claim her as an old friend. She was as glad to see these little birds as they were to see her, and she welcomed them by holding out both her hands. Thereupon they all tried to alight on her two hands, crowding one another off, with a great fluttering of their wings. One dear little bird nestled close to her and another put its bill to her lips.

Violet and Peony stood laughing at this pretty sight, for they enjoyed the merry time their playmate was having as much as if they were taking part in it.

"Violet," said her mother, "tell me the truth, who is this little girl?"

"My darling Mamma," answered Violet, "I have told you truly who she is. It is our little snow-image which Peony and I have been making. Peony will tell you so as well as I."

"Yes, Mamma," said Peony, "this is our little snow-child. Is she not a nice one? But Mamma, her hand is very cold!"

Just then the street gate opened and the father appeared with a fur cap drawn down over his ears, and the thickest of gloves upon his hands. His eyes brightened at the sight of his wife and children, but he was surprised to find the whole family in the open air. Then he saw a little white stranger sporting to and fro in the garden, like a dancing snow-wreath, with a flock of snowbirds fluttering about her head.

"What little girl may that be?" asked their father. "Her mother must be crazy to let her go out in such bitter weather with only that thin white gown and those thin slippers!"

"My dear husband," said his wife, "I know nothing about the little thing. She is some neighbor's child, I suppose. Our Violet and Peony insist that she is only a snow-image, which they have been making in the garden."

"Father, do you see how it is? This is our snow-image which Peony and I have made, because we wanted another playmate. Did we not, Peony?" said Violet.

"Yes, Papa," said Peony. "This be our little snow-sister. Is she not beau-ti-ful? But she gave such a cold kiss!"

"Nonsense, children," cried their father. "Come, wife, this little stranger must not stay out here in the cold a moment longer. We will take her into the parlor and you shall give her a supper of warm bread and milk. Meanwhile I will give notice among the neighbors of a lost child."

So saying, he went toward the white

figure. But Violet and Peony seized him by the hand and begged him not to make her come in.

"Dear Father," cried Violet, putting herself before him, "it is true what I have been telling you! This is our little snow-girl and she can only live in the cold west wind. Do not make her come into the hot room."

"Yes, Father," shouted Peony, stamping his little foot, "this be nothing but our little snow-child. She will not love the hot fire."

"Nonsense, children, nonsense!" cried the father. "Run into the house this moment. It is too late to play any longer now. I must take care of this little girl or she will catch her death of cold."

The father entered the garden, breaking away from his two children. They sent their shrill voices after him, begging him to let the snow-child stay and enjoy herself in the cold west wind. As he came near, the snow-birds took flight and the little white figure flew backwards, shaking her head as if to say, "Do not touch me!"

Once the good man stumbled and fell. Some of the neighbors saw him from their windows and wondered why he was running about his garden after a snowdrift, which the west wind was driving hither and thither. At length he chased the little stranger into a corner, where she could not get away from him.

"Come, you odd little thing!" cried he, seizing her by the hand, "I have caught you at last. We will put a nice pair of warm stockings on your little feet, and you shall be wrapped in a shawl. Your poor white nose is frostbitten, but we will make it all right. Come along in."

The little white figure followed him sadly, for all her glow and sparkle was gone. She looked as dull and limp as a thaw. As the father led her up the steps to the door Violet and Peony looked into his face. Their eyes were full of tears, and again they begged him not to bring the little snow-image into the house.

"Not bring her in!" cried the kind-hearted man. "Why, you are crazy, my little

Violet—quite crazy, my small Peony! She is so cold that her hand has almost frozen mine. Would you have her freeze to death?"

"After all," said the mother, who had been looking at the child earnestly, "she does look like a snow-image! I do believe she is made of snow!" A puff of the west wind blew against the snow-child and again she sparkled like a star.

"Snow!" repeated the father, "no wonder she looks like snow! She is half frozen, poor little thing! But a good fire will make everything right."

Then he led the little white figure out of the frosty air into the warm parlor. A stove filled with coal sent a bright gleam through the room. The parlor was hung with red curtains and covered with a red carpet and looked just as warm as it felt.

The father placed the child on the hearth rug in front of the stove.

"Now she will be warm," said he, rubbing his hands and looking about pleasantly. "Make yourself at home, my child."

The little white maiden looked sad and drooping, as she stood on the hearth rug. Once she glanced toward the windows and saw the white roofs outside. The cold wind rattled the window panes as if it were telling her to come out. But there stood the snow-child drooping before the hot stove.

The father saw nothing amiss. "Come, wife," said he, "let her have a pair of thick stockings and a woolen shawl and give her some warm supper as soon as the milk boils. Violet and Peony, amuse your little friend and I will go among the neighbors to find out where she belongs."

Without listening to his two children, who still kept saying that their little snow-sister did not like the warmth, the father went out, shutting the door carefully behind him. Turning up the collar of his coat he left the house. He had barely reached the gate when he was recalled by the scream of Violet and Peony, and a rapping on the window.

"Husband, husband!" cried his wife,

"there is no need of looking for her parents."

"We told you so, Father!" cried Violet and Peony, as he re-entered the parlor. "You would bring her in, and now poor, dear, beautiful little snow-sister is thawed!"

The father felt anxious lest his children might thaw, too, and he asked his wife to explain. She said, "I was called to the parlor by the cries of Violet and Peony. I found no trace of the little white maiden, unless it was a heap of snow which melted on the hearth rug. There you see all that is left of it," added she, pointing to a pool of water in front of the stove.

"Yes, Father," said Violet, through her tears, "that is all that is left of our dear little snow-sister."

—*Arranged from Nathaniel Hawthorne.*

A Visit from St. Nicholas

'Twas the night before Christmas,
    when all through the house
Not a creature was stirring,
    not even a mouse;

The stockings were hung
    by the chimney with care,

In hopes that St. Nicholas
    soon would be there.

The children were nestled
    all snug in their beds,
While visions of sugar-plums
    danced in their heads;

And Mamma in her kerchief,
    and I in my cap,
Had just settled our brains
    for a long winter's nap,

When out on the lawn
    there arose such a clatter,
I sprang from my bed
    to see what was the matter.

Away to the window
    I flew like a flash,
Tore open the shutter
    and threw up the sash.

The moon, on the breast
    of the new-fallen snow,
Gave a lustre of midday
    to objects below;

When, what to my wondering
    eyes should appear,
But a miniature sleigh
    and eight tiny reindeer,

With a little old driver,
    so lively and quick,
I knew in a moment
    it must be St. Nick!

More rapid than eagles
    his coursers they came,
And he whistled, and shouted,
    and called them by name:

"Now, Dasher! Now, Dancer, now,
    Prancer and Vixen!
On, Comet! on, Cupid!
    on, Dunder and Blitzen!

To the top of the porch,
    to the top of the wall,
Now, dash away, dash away,
    dash away, all!"

As dry leaves that before
    the wild hurricane fly,

When they meet with an obstacle,
    mount to the sky,

So, up to the house-top
    the coursers they flew,
With the sleigh full of toys—
    and St. Nicholas, too.

And then in a twinkling,
    I heard on the roof
The prancing and pawing
    of each little hoof.

As I drew in my head,
    and was turning around,
Down the chimney St. Nicholas
    came with a bound.

He was dressed all in fur
    from his head to his foot,
And his clothes were all tarnished
    with ashes and soot;

A bundle of toys he had flung
    on his back,
And he looked like a peddler
    just opening his pack.

His eyes, how they twinkled!
 his dimples, how merry!
His cheeks were like roses,
 his nose like a cherry;

His droll little mouth was
 drawn up like a bow,
And the beard on his chin was
 as white as the snow.

The stump of a pipe he held
 tight in his teeth,
And the smoke it encircled
 his head like a wreath.

He had a broad face
 and a little round belly
That shook, when he laughed,
 like a bowl full of jelly.

He was chubby and plump—
 a right jolly old elf:
And I laughed when I saw him,
 in spite of myself.

A wink of his eye,
 and a twist of his head,

Soon gave me to know
    I had nothing to dread.

He spoke not a word,
    but went straight to his work,
And filled all the stockings;
    then turned with a jerk,

And laying his finger
    aside of his nose,
And giving a nod,
    up the chimney he rose.

He sprang to his sleigh,
    to his team gave a whistle,
And away they all flew
    like the down of a thistle.

But I heard him exclaim,
    ere he drove out of sight,
"Happy Christmas to all,
    and to all a good night!"

—Clement C. Moore.

A Dog of Flanders

Nello and Patrasche were friends.

They were both of the same age. They had dwelt together almost all their days and they loved each other very dearly.

Their home was a little hut on the edge of a small village not far from Antwerp. The village was set in broad pastures with long lines of poplars and of alders along the great canal which ran through it. It had about a score of houses with shutters of bright green or sky-blue, and roofs rose-red or black and white, and walls whitewashed, until they shone in the sun like snow.

In the center of the village stood a windmill. Opposite the windmill was the little old gray church, whose bell rang morning, noon and night.

Within sound of the little bell, Nello and Patrasche lived in the little hut. It was the home of a very old man who had been a soldier. A wound had made him a cripple.

When this old man was eighty, his daughter died and left him her two year old son, Nello. The old man and the little child lived contentedly in the poor little hut.

It was a humble mud hut, but it was clean and white as a seashell. It stood in a small garden where they raised beans and herbs and pumpkins. They were very poor. Many a day they had scarcely anything to eat. But the old man was gentle and good to the boy, and the boy was a beautiful, truthful lad. They were happy on a crust and a few leaves of cabbage and asked for nothing except that Patrasche should be always with them.

For Patrasche was their breadwinner, their only friend and comforter. Patrasche was hands, head and feet to both of them. He was their very life, for the man was old and a cripple and Nello was but a child, and Patrasche was their dog.

Patrasche was a dog of Flanders with yellow hide and a large head, with wolf-like ears that stood erect, and bowed legs. He came of a race which had toiled hard for many a century.

Before he was thirteen months old he was sold to a hardware dealer, who wandered over the land, north and south, from the blue sea to the green mountains. He had been sold for a small price because he was so young. His new master was sullen, selfish and cruel. He heaped his cart full with pots and pans, and flagons and buckets, and other wares. Then he left Patrasche to draw the load as best he could.

One day, after two years of this toil, Patrasche was going along one of the dusty roads. It was full midsummer, and very warm. His cart was heavy and his owner walked on without noticing him. Going along thus in the full sun, and not having tasted water for twelve hours, Patrasche staggered and fell.

He fell in the middle of the dusty road, in the full glare of the sun. Patrasche lay in the summer dust as if dead, so his master kicked his body into the grass. He lay there in the grass-grown ditch. It was a busy road and hundreds of people went by, on foot and on mules, in wagons and in carts.

After a time there came along a little old man who was bent and lame and very feeble. He looked at Patrasche and turned aside. Then he knelt down in the grass and weeds and looked at the dog with eyes of pity. There was with him a little rosy, dark-eyed child who stood gazing upon the poor dog.

Thus it was that the little Nello and the big Patrasche met for the first time.

The old man drew the dog home to his own little hut, which was a stone's throw among the fields. There he tended him with so much care that the sickness, which had been brought on by heat and thirst, passed away. Health and strength returned, and Patrasche staggered up again upon his four stout legs.

For many weeks he had been useless, but all this time he had heard no rough word, and had felt no harsh touch. He had heard only the little child's voice and felt the caress of the old man's hand.

During the dog's sickness this lonely old man and the happy little child had grown to care for him. He had a corner of the hut with a heap of dry grass for his bed. When he was well enough to give a loud bark, they laughed aloud and almost wept for joy. Little Nello hung chains of flowers round his neck and kissed him.

So when Patrasche arose again, strong and big and powerful, his great eyes had a gentle surprise in them. There were no curses to arouse him, and no blows to drive him, and his heart awakened to a great love which never failed. Patrasche was grateful. He lay with grave, tender eyes watching his friends.

Now, the old soldier could do nothing for his living but limp about with a small cart. In this cart he carried the milk cans of his neighbors into the town of Antwerp. But it was hard work for the old man. He was eighty-three, and Antwerp was a good league off.

Patrasche watched the milk cans come and go that first day when he got well. He was lying in the sun with the wreath of flowers around his neck.

The next morning, before the old man had touched the cart, Patrasche arose and walked to it. He placed himself between its handles and showed his wish to work in return for the bread he had eaten. When they did not harness him, he tried to draw the cart with his teeth.

At length the old man made his cart so that Patrasche could walk between the handles and pull it. This the dog did every morning of his life thereafter.

When winter came, the old man thanked the fortune that had brought him the dog, for he was very old and he grew more feeble each year. He could not have taken his load of milk cans over the snow and through the mud if it had not been for the strength of this dog.

As for Patrasche, it seemed heaven to him. It was nothing but play to step out with this little green cart with its bright brass cans, and to walk by the side of the gentle old man. Besides, his work was over by three or four o'clock in the day, and after that time he was free to do as he would. He could stretch himself, sleep in the sun, wander in the fields, romp with the young child, or play with the other dogs. Patrasche was happy.

A few years later the old man became so lame that he could not go out with the cart any more. Then little Nello, who was now six years of age, took his place beside the cart. He sold the milk and brought back the coins to their owners with a pretty grace that charmed all who saw him.

Many an artist sketched the group as it went by him, the green cart with the brass cans, and the great dog with his belled harness, and the small boy with his little white feet in great wooden shoes.

Nello and Patrasche did the work so well that when the summer came the old man had no need to stir out. He could sit in the doorway in the sun and see them go forth through the garden. Then he would doze, and dream, and pray a little, and then awake again as the clock tolled three and watch for their return.

On their return Patrasche would shake himself free of his harness with a bay of glee, and Nello would tell with pride the doings of the day. Then they would all go in to their meal of rye-bread and milk or soup, and watch the shadows over the plain. After that they would lie down to sleep while the old man said a prayer.

So the days and years went on, and the lives of Nello and Patrasche were happy. They were never heard to complain. The child's wooden shoes and the dog's four legs would trot together over the frozen field to the chime of the bells on the harness.

Sometimes in the streets of Antwerp, some housewife would bring them a bowl of soup and a handful of bread, or some woman in their own village would bid them keep some of the milk for their own food. Then they would run over the white lands through the early darkness, bright and happy, and burst with a shout of joy into their home.

Patrasche in his heart was grateful. Though he was often hungry; though he had to work in the heat of summer and the chill of winter; though his feet were often cut by the sharp stones or ice; yet he was grateful and content. He did his duty with each day, and the eyes that he loved smiled down on him. That was enough for Patrasche.

—Adapted from Ouida's "A Dog of Flanders."

Robin Redbreast

Good-by, good-by to Summer!
    For Summer's nearly done;
The garden smiling faintly,
    Cool breezes in the sun:
Our Thrushes now are silent,
    Our Swallows flown away,—
But Robin's here, in coat of brown,
    With ruddy breast-knot gay.

Robin, Robin Redbreast,
    O Robin dear!
Robin singing sweetly
    In the falling of the year.

Bright yellow, red, and orange,
    The leaves come down in hosts;
The trees are Indian Princes,
    But soon they'll turn to Ghosts;

The scanty pears and apples
    Hang russet on the bough,
It's Autumn, Autumn, Autumn late,
    'Twill soon be Winter now.

Robin, Robin Redbreast,
    O Robin dear!
And welaway! my Robin,
    For pinching tinges are near.

The fireside for the Cricket,
    The wheatstack for the Mouse,
When trembling night-winds whistle
    And moan all round the house;

The frosty ways like iron,
    The brandies plumed with snow,—
Alas! in Winter, dead and dark,
    Where can poor Robin go?

Robin, Robin Redbreast,
    O Robin dear!
And a crumb of bread for Robin,
    His little heart to cheer.

                —William Allingham.

Little Gustava

Little Gustava sits in the sun,
Safe in the porch, and the little drops run
From the icicles under the eaves so fast,
For the bright spring sun shines warm at last,
    And glad is little Gustava.

She wears a quaint little scarlet cap,
And a little green bowl she holds in her lap,
Filled with bread and milk to the brim,
And a wreath of marigolds round the rim;
    "Ha, ha!" laughs little Gustava.

Up comes her little gray coaxing cat,
With her little pink nose, and she mews:
    "What's that?"
Gustava feeds her—she begs for more;
And a little brown hen walks in at the door;
    "Good day!" cries little Gustava.

She scatters crumbs for the little brown hen;
There comes a rush and a flutter, and then
Down fly her little white doves, so sweet,
With their snowy wings and their crimson
    feet;
    "Welcome," cries little Gustava.

So dainty and eager, they pick up the crumbs,
But who is this through the doorway comes?
Little Scotch terrier, little dog Rags
Looks in her face, and his funny tail wags;
   "Ha, ha!" laughs little Gustava.

"You want some breakfast, too?" and down
She sets her bowl on the brick floor brown;
And her little dog Rags drinks up her milk,
While she strokes his shaggy locks like silk;
   "Dear Rags!" says little Gustava.

Waiting without, stood sparrow and crow,
Cooling their feet in the melting snow;
"Won't you come in, good folk?" she cried.
But they were too bashful, and stayed outside,
   Though "Pray come in!" cried Gustava.

So the last she threw them, and knelt on the mat
With doves and biddy and dog and cat.
And her mother came to the open house door:
"Dear little daughter, I bring you some more,
   My merry little Gustava!"

—Celia Thaxter.

Good Night and Good Morning

A fair little girl sat under a tree,
Sewing as long as her eyes could see;
Then smoothed her work and folded it right,
And said, "Dear work, good night, good night!"

Such a number of rooks came over her head,
Crying "Caw! caw!" on their way to bed,
She said, as she watched their curious flight,
"Little black things, good night, good night!"

The horses neighed, and the oxen lowed,
The sheep's "bleat! bleat!" came over the
    road;
All seeming to say, with a quiet delight,
"Good little girl, good night, good night!"

She did not say to the sun, "good night!"
Though she saw him there like a ball of
    light;
For she knew he had God's own time to keep
All over the world, and never could sleep.

The tall pink foxglove bowed his head;
The violets curtsied, and went to bed;
And good little Lucy tied up her hair,
And said, on her knees, her favorite prayer.

And while on her pillow she softly lay,
She knew nothing more till again it was day;
And all things said to the beautiful sun,
"Good morning, good morning! Our work is
    begun."

—Lord Houghton.

How Doth the Little Busy Bee

How doth the little busy bee
    Improve each shining hour,
And gather honey all the day
    From every opening flower.

How skillfully she builds her cell;
    How neat she spreads her wax,
And labors hard to store it well
    With the sweet food she makes.

In works of labor or of skill
    I would be busy too;
For Satan finds some mischief still
    For idle hands to do.

In books, or work, or healthful play,
    Let my first years be passed;
That I may give for every day
    Some good account at last.

—Isaac Watts.

The Bluebird

I know the song that the bluebird is singing,
Out in the apple-tree where he is swinging.
Brave little fellow! The skies may be dreary,
Nothing cares he while his heart is so
      cheery.

Hark! how the music leaps out from his
      throat!
Hark! was there ever so merry a note?
Listen awhile, and you'll hear what he's
      saying,
Up in the apple-tree, swinging and swaying:

"Dear little blossoms, down under the snow,
You must be weary of winter, I know;
Hark! while I sing you a message of cheer,
Summer is coming and springtime is here!

"Little white snowdrop, I pray you arise;
Bright yellow crocus, come, open your eyes;
Sweet little violets hid from the cold,
Put on your mantles of purple and gold;
Daffodils, daffodils! say, do you hear?
Summer is coming, and springtime is here!"

            —Mrs. *Emily Huntington Miller.*

Answer to a Child's Question

Do you ask what the birds say? The
    sparrow, the dove,
The linnet and thrush say, "I love! and
    I love!"
In the winter they're silent—the wind is
    so strong;
What it says I don't know, but it sings a
    loud song.
But green leaves and blossoms and
    sunny, warm weather
And singing and loving—all come back
    together.
But the lark is so brimful of gladness
    and love,
The green fields below him, the blue
    sky above,
That he sings, and he sings; and forever
    sings he—
"I love my Love, and my Love loves me!"

    —*Samuel Taylor Coleridge.*

Black Beauty

The first place that I can remember was a pleasant meadow with a pond of clear water in it. Some shady trees leaned over it, and rushes and water-lilies grew at the deep end. At the top of the meadow was a grove of fir trees, and at the bottom a running brook was overhung by a steep bank.

There were six young colts in the meadow beside me. I used to run with them, and had great fun. We used to gallop round and round the field as hard as we could go. Sometimes we had rough play, for we would bite and kick as well as gallop.

One day, when there was a great deal of kicking, my mother whinnied to me to come to her, and then she said:

"I wish you to pay attention to what I am going to say to you. You have been well-bred and well-born; your father has a great name in these parts; your grandmother had the sweetest temper of any horse I ever knew, and I think you have never seen me kick or bite. I hope you will grow up gentle and good, and never learn bad ways. Do your work with a good will, lift your feet up well when you trot, and never bite or kick even in play."

I have never forgotten my mother's advice.

Our master was a good, kind man. He

gave us good food, good lodging, and kind words; he spoke as kindly to us as he did to his little children. We were all fond of him, and my mother loved him very much. When she saw him at the gate she would neigh with joy and trot up to him. He would pat and stroke her and say, "Well, old Pet, and how is your little Darkie?" I was a dull black, so he called me Darkie. Then he would give me a piece of bread which was very good, and sometimes he brought a carrot for my mother.

There was a plowboy, Dick, who sometimes came into our field to pluck blackberries from the hedge. When he had eaten all he wanted he would have what he called fun with the colts, throwing stones and sticks at them to make them gallop. We did not mind him much, for we could gallop off; but sometimes a stone would hit and hurt us.

One day he was at this game and did not know that the master was in the next field watching what was going on. As soon as we saw the master we trotted up nearer to the side of the field to see what happened.

"Bad boy!" he said, "bad boy! to chase the colts. This is not the first time, nor the second, but it shall be the last. Take your money and go home; I shall not want you on my farm again." So we never saw Dick any more.

My master would not sell me till I was four years old. He said lads ought not to work like men, and colts ought not to work like horses till they were quite grown up.

When I was four years old Squire Gordon came to look at me. I was now growing handsome; my coat was fine and soft, and was bright black. I had one white foot and a pretty white star on my forehead. He examined my eyes, my mouth, and my legs. Then I had to walk and trot and gallop before him. He seemed to like me and said, "When he has been well broken in he will do very well." My master said he would break me in himself, as he did not wish me to be frightened or hurt. He lost no time about it, for the next day he began.

"Breaking in" means to teach a horse to wear a saddle and bridle, and to carry on his back a man, woman, or child; to go just the way desired, and to go quietly. Besides this he has to learn to wear harness, and to stand still while it is put on. Then he has a cart or a carriage fixed behind, so that he cannot walk or trot without dragging it after him; and he must go fast or slow, just as his driver wishes. He must never start at what he sees, nor speak to other horses, nor bite, nor kick; nor have any will of his own; but he must always do his master's will, even though he may be very tired or hungry. But the worst of all is, when his harness is once on, he may neither jump for joy nor lie down for weariness. So you see this "breaking in" is a great thing.

I had, of course, long been used to a halter and a headstall, and to being led about in the fields and lanes quietly; but now I was to have a bit and bridle. My master gave me some oats, and after much coaxing he got the bit into my mouth, and the bridle fixed, but it was a nasty thing!

One who has never had a bit in his mouth cannot think how it feels. A great piece of cold, hard steel as thick as a man's finger is pushed into the mouth, between the teeth, and over the tongue, with the ends coming out at the corner of the mouth. It is held fast there by straps over the head, under the throat, round the nose and under the chin.

It is bad! yes, very bad! but I knew my mother always wore a bit when she went out, and all horses did when they were grown up; and so, with the nice oats, and my master's pats, kind words and gentle ways, I got to wear my bit and bridle.

Next came the saddle, but that was not half so bad. My master put it on my back very gently; he then made the girths fast under my body, patting and talking to me all the time. Then I had a few oats, then a little leading about. This he did every day till I began to look for the oats and the saddle. One morning my master got on my back and rode me round the meadow on the soft grass. It certainly did feel queer;

but I must say I felt proud to carry my master. He rode me a little every day and I soon became used to it.

The next thing was putting on the iron shoes; that, too, was very hard at first. My master went with me to the smith's forge, to see that I was not hurt or frightened. The blacksmith took my feet in his hand, one after the other, and cut away some of the hoof. It did not pain me, so I stood still on three legs till he had done them all. Then he took a piece of iron the shape of my foot, and clapped it on, and drove some nails through the shoe into my hoof, so that the shoe was firmly on. My feet felt very stiff and heavy, but in time I got used to it.

And now my master went on to break me to harness. First a stiff, heavy collar was put on my neck, and a bridle with great side-pieces against my eyes called blinkers. And blinkers indeed they were, for I could not see on either side, but only straight in front of me. Next there was a small saddle with a stiff strap that went around my tail;

that was the crupper. I hated the crupper; to have my long tail doubled up and poked through that strap was almost as bad as the bit. I never felt more like kicking, but I could not kick such a good master. In time I got used to everything, and could do my work as well as my mother.

Then my master sent me for a fortnight to a meadow which was near a railway. Here were some sheep and cows, and I was turned in among them.

I shall never forget the first train that ran by. I was feeding quietly near the pales which separated the meadow from the railway, when I heard a strange sound. Before I knew whence it came—with a rush and a clatter, and a puffing out of smoke—a long black train flew by, and was gone almost before I could draw my breath. I turned and galloped to the other side of the meadow as fast as I could go, and there I stood snorting with fear.

During the day many other trains went by, some more slowly; these drew up at the station close by, and sometimes made an awful shriek and groan before they stopped. I thought it dreadful, but the cows went on eating, and hardly raised their heads as the black thing came puffing and grinding past.

For the first few days I could not feed in peace; but as I found that this creature never came into the field, nor did me any harm, very soon I cared as little about the passing of a train as did the cows and sheep. Thanks to my good master's care, I am as fearless at railway stations as in my own stable.

My master often drove me in double harness with my mother, because she was steady and could teach me how to go better than a strange horse. She told me the better I behaved the better I should be treated, and that it was always best to please my master. "But," said she, "there are many kinds of men; there are good, thoughtful men like our master, that any horse may be proud to serve; and there are bad men, who never ought to have a horse or a dog to call their own. I hope you will fall into good hands; but a horse never knows who may buy him, or who may drive him. Still I say, do your best wherever it is, and keep up your good name."

It was early in May, when there came a man from Squire Gordon's, who took me away. My master said, "Good-by, Darkie; be a good horse, and always do your best." I could not say "good-by," so I put my nose into his hand. He patted me kindly, and I left my first home.

—*Adapted from "Black Beauty" by Anna Sewell.*

Ginger

Ginger was a tall chestnut mare with a long, handsome neck. She stood in the stall just beyond mine. The first day I was in my new home she looked across to me and said:

"So it is you who have turned me out of my box; it is a very strange thing for a colt like you to come and turn a lady out of her own home."

"I beg your pardon," I said, "I have turned no one out; the man who brought me put me here, and I had nothing to do with it. As to my being a colt, I am turned four years old and am a grown-up horse. I never had words yet with horse or mare, and it is my wish to live at peace."

"Well," she said, "we shall see. Of course, I do not want to have words with a young thing like you." I said no more.

A few days after this I had to go out with Ginger in the carriage. I wondered how we should get on together; but except laying her ears back when I was led up to her, she behaved very well. She did her work honestly, and did her full share, and I never wish to have a better partner. When we came to a hill she would throw her weight into the collar and pull away. We had the same courage at our work and our master never had to use the whip on either of us. Then our paces were much the same, and I found it easy to keep step with her when trotting. After we had been out two or three times together we grew quite friendly, which made me feel very much at home.

One day when Ginger and I were standing alone in the shade she wanted to know all about my bringing up and breaking in, and I told her.

"Well," said she, "if I had had your bringing up, I might have had as good a temper as you, but now I don't believe I ever shall."

"Why not?" I said.

"Because it has been all so different with me," she replied. "I never had any one, horse or man, that was kind to me, or that I cared to please. In the first place I was taken from my mother as soon as I was weaned, and put with a lot of other young colts. None of them cared for me, and I cared for none of them.

"There was no kind master like yours to look after me, and talk to me, and bring me nice things to eat. The man that had the care of us never gave me a kind word in my life. I do not mean that he ill-used me, but he did not care for us one bit further than to see that we had plenty to eat, and shelter in the winter.

"A footpath ran through our field, and very often the boys passing through would fling stones to make us gallop. I was never hit, but one fine young colt was badly cut in the face, and he was scarred for life. We did not care for them, but of course it made us more wild, and we felt that boys were our enemies.

"We had fun in the meadows, galloping up and down and chasing each other round and round the field; then standing still under the shade of the trees. But when it came to 'breaking in,' that was a bad time for me. Several men came to catch me, and when at last they closed me in at one corner of the field, one caught me by the forelock. Another caught me by the nose and held it so tight I could hardly draw my breath. Then another took my under jaw in his hard hand and wrenched my mouth open, and so they got the halter on and the bit into my mouth. Then one dragged me along by the halter, another flogging behind.

"They did not give me a chance to know what they wanted. I was high-bred and had a great deal of spirit. I was very wild, and gave them plenty of trouble; but it was dreadful to be shut up in a stall day after day, and I fretted and pined and wanted to get loose.

"My old master could have done anything with me, but he had given up all the hard part of the work to his son and he came only at times to oversee. His son was a strong, tall, bold man; they called him Samson, and he used to boast that he had never found a horse that could throw him. There was no gentleness in him, as there was in his father, but only hardness, a hard voice, a hard eye, a hard hand. I felt from the first that he wanted to wear all the spirit out of me, and just make me into a quiet, obedient piece of horseflesh. 'Horseflesh!' Yes, that is all that he thought about." And Ginger stamped her foot as if the very thought of him made her angry. Then she went on:

"If I did not do exactly what he wanted he would make me run round the training field till he had tired me out. One day he had worked me hard, and when I lay down I was tired and angry, and it all seemed so hard.

"The next morning he came for me early, and ran me round again for a long time. I had scarcely had an hour's rest when he came again for me with a saddle and bridle and a new kind of bit. He had just mounted me when something I did put him out of temper, and he chucked me hard with the rein.

"The new bit was very painful, and I reared up suddenly, which angered him still more, and he began to flog me. I felt my whole spirit set against him, and I began to kick, and plunge, and rear, as I had never done before, and we had a regular fight. For a long time he stuck to the saddle and punished me cruelly with his whip and spurs. My blood was up, and I cared for nothing he could do if I could only get him off.

"At last after a hard struggle I threw him off backward. I heard him fall heavily on the turf, and without looking behind me I galloped off to the other end of the field. There I turned round and saw him slowly rising and going into the stable. I stood under an oak tree and watched, but no one came to catch me.

"Time went on and the sun was very hot. The flies swarmed round me and settled on my bleeding flanks where the spurs had dug in. I felt hungry, for I had not eaten since the early morning, but there was not enough grass in that meadow for a goose to live on. I wanted to lie down and rest, but with the saddle strapped on there was no comfort, and there was not a drop of water to drink. The afternoon wore on, and the sun got low. I saw the other colts led in, and I knew they were having a good feed.

"At last, just as the sun went down, I saw my old master come out with a sieve in his hand. He was a fine old gentleman with white hair, but his voice was what I should know him by among a thousand. It was not high, nor yet low, but full and clear and kind, and when he gave orders it was so steady and decided every one knew, both horses and men, that he must be obeyed.

"He came quietly along, now and then shaking the oats he had in the sieve, and speaking cheerfully and gently to me: 'Come along, lassie, come along, lassie; come along.' I stood still and let him come up; he held the oats to me, and I began to eat without fear; his voice took all my fear away. He stood by, patting and stroking me while I was eating.

"When he saw the clots of blood on my side he seemed much vexed. 'Poor lassie! it was a bad business, a bad business.' Then he quietly took the rein and led me to the stable. Just at the door stood Samson. I laid my ears back and snapped at him. 'Stand back,' said the master, 'and keep out of her way; you've done a bad day's work for this filly.' He growled out something about an ugly brute. 'Hark ye,' said the father, 'a bad-tempered man will never make a good-tempered horse. You've not learned your trade yet, Samson.'

"Then he led me into my box, took off the saddle and bridle with his own hands and tied me up. He called for a pail of warm water and a sponge, took off his coat, and sponged my sides a good while, so tenderly that I was sure he knew how sore and bruised they were. 'Whoa! my pretty one,' he said, 'stand still, stand still.' Even his voice did me good, and the bathing was very comfortable.

"The skin was so broken at the corners of my mouth that I could not eat the hay. He looked closely at it, shook his head, and told the man to make a good bran mash and put some meal into it. How good that mash was! and so soft and healing to my mouth. He stood by all the time I was eating, stroking me and talking to the man. 'If a fine horse like this,' said he, 'cannot be broken by fair means, she will never be good for anything.'

"After that he often came to see me, and when my mouth was healed the other breaker went on training me; he was steady and thoughtful, and I soon learned what he wanted."

The next time that Ginger and I were together in the paddock she told me about her first place.

"After my breaking in," she said, "I was bought by a dealer to match another chestnut horse, sent up to London. I had been driven with a check-rein, and I hated it worse than anything else. But in this place we were reined far tighter, the coachman and his master thinking we looked more stylish so.

"I like to toss my head about and hold it as high as any horse. But it was cruel to be obliged to hold it high for hours. Besides that, I had to have two bits instead of one. They hurt my tongue and my jaw. It was worst when we had to stand by the hour waiting for our mistress at some grand party. If I fretted or stamped the whip was laid on. It was enough to drive one mad."

"Did not your master take any thought for you?" I said.

"No," said she, "he cared only to have a stylish turnout; I think he knew very little about horses. He left that to his coachman, who told him I had a bad temper. I was willing to work, and ready to work hard, too, but not to be tormented for nothing. What right had they to make me suffer like that? Besides the soreness in my mouth, and the pain in my neck, it made my windpipe feel bad. If I had stopped there long I know it would have spoiled my breathing.

"I grew more and more restless and fretful. I could not help it, and I began to snap and kick when any one came to harness me. For this the groom beat me, and one day, as they had just buckled us into the carriage and were straining my head up with that rein, I began to plunge and kick with all my might. I soon broke a lot of harness, and kicked myself clear; so that was an end of that place.

"After this I was again sold. My new master tried me in all kinds of ways and with different bits, and he soon found out what I could not bear. At last he drove me without a check-rein, and then sold me, as a quiet horse to a gentleman in the country. He was a good master, and I was getting on very well, but his old groom left him and a new one came.

"The new groom was as hard-tempered and hard-handed as Samson. He always spoke in a harsh voice. If I did not move in the stall the moment he wanted me, he hit me with his stable broom or fork. Everything he did was rough, and I began to hate him. He wanted to make me afraid of him, but I was too high-mettled for that.

"One day, when he had mistreated me more than usual, I bit him, and he began to hit me about the head with a riding whip. After that he never dared to come into my stall again. Either my heels or my teeth were ready for him, and he knew it. My master listened to what the man said, and so I was sold again.

"The same dealer heard of me, and said he thought he knew one place where I would do well. 'It was a pity,' he said, 'that such a fine horse should go to the bad for want of a good chance,' and the end of it was that I came here not long before you did. But I had made up my mind that men were my enemies and that I must defend myself. I wish I could think about things as you do; but I can't, after all I have gone through."

I was sorry for Ginger, but I thought she had made the worst of it. However, I found as the weeks went on, she grew more gentle and cheerful. She lost that watchful, hard look.

One day the groom said, "I do believe that mare is getting fond of me, she whinnied this morning when I had been rubbing her forehead."

Master saw the change, too, and one day

when he got out of the carriage and came to speak to us he stroked her beautiful neck. "Well, my pretty one, how do things go with you now? You are much happier than when you came to us, I think."

She put her nose up to him in a friendly, trustful way, while he rubbed it gently.

"We shall make a cure of her," he said.

"Yes, sir; she's wonderfully improved," said the groom, "she's not the same creature that she was. She will be as good as Black Beauty by and by. Kindness is all she needs, poor thing. One pound of patience and gentleness, firmness and petting, mixed with half a pint of common sense, and given to the horse every day, will cure almost any vicious animal."

—Adapted from "Black Beauty," by Anna Sewell.

The Spider and the Fly

"Will you walk into my parlor?"
   said the Spider to the Fly,
" 'Tis the prettiest little parlor
   that ever you did spy;
The way into my parlor
   is up a winding stair,
And I have many curious things
   to show when you are there."

"Oh no, no," said the little Fly,
   "to ask me is in vain;
For who goes up your winding stair
   can ne'er come down again."

"I'm sure you must be weary, dear,
    with soaring up so high;
Will you rest upon my little bed?"
    said the Spider to the Fly.
"There are pretty curtains drawn around,
    the sheets are fine and thin,
And if you like to rest awhile,
    I'll snugly tuck you in!"
"Oh no, no," said the little Fly,
    "for I've often heard it said,
They never, never wake again,
    who sleep upon your bed!"

Said the cunning Spider to the Fly,
    "Dear friend, what can I do
To prove the warm affection
    I've always felt for you?
I have, within my pantry,
    good store of all that's nice;
I'm sure you're very welcome—
    will you please to take a slice?"
"Oh no, no," said the little Fly,
    "kind sir, that cannot be,
I've heard what's in your pantry,
    and I do not wish to see!"

"Sweet creature," said the Spider,
    "you're witty and you're wise;
How handsome are your gauzy wings,
    how brilliant are your eyes!
I have a little looking glass
    upon my parlor shelf;
If you'll step in one moment, dear,
    you shall behold yourself."
"I thank you, gentle sir," she said,
    "for what you're pleased to say,
And bidding you good morning now,
    I'll call another day."

The Spider turned him round about,
    and went into his den,
For well he knew the silly Fly
    would soon be back again;
So he wove a subtle web
    in a little corner sly,
And set his table ready
    to dine upon the Fly.
Then he came out to his door again,
    and merrily did sing,—
"Come hither, hither, pretty Fly,
    with the pearl and silver wing;

Your robes are green and purple,
    there's a crest upon your head;
Your eyes are like the diamond bright,
    but mine are dull as lead."

Alas, alas! how very soon
    this silly little Fly,
Hearing his wily, flattering words,
    came slowly flitting by:
With buzzing wings she hung aloft,
    then near and nearer drew,—
Thinking only of her brilliant eyes,
    and green and purple hue;
Thinking only of her crested head—
    poor foolish thing! At last,
Up jumped the cunning Spider,
    and fiercely held her fast,
He dragged her up his winding stair,
    into his dismal den
Within his little parlor—but she
    ne'er came out again!

—Mary Howitt.

The Owl and the Pussy-Cat

The Owl and the Pussy-Cat went to sea
    In a beautiful pea-green boat;
They took some honey, and plenty of money
    Wrapped up in a five-pound note.
The Owl looked up to the moon above,
    And sang to a small guitar,
"O lovely Pussy! O Pussy, my love,
    What a beautiful Pussy you are,—
        You are,
What a beautiful Pussy you are!"

Pussy said to the Owl, "You elegant fowl!
    How wonderful sweet you sing!
O let us be married,—too long we have
        tarried,—
    But what shall we do for a ring?"

They sailed away for a year and a day
    To the land where the Bong tree grows;
And there in a wood, a piggy-wig stood
    With a ring at the end of his nose,—
        His nose,
With a ring at the end of his nose.

"Dear Pig, are you willing to sell for one
        shilling
    Your ring?" Said the piggy, "I will."
So they took it away, and were married
        next day
    By the Turkey who lives on the hill.

They dined upon mince and slices of quince,
    Which they ate with a runcible spoon,
And hand in hand on the edge of the sand
    They danced by the light of the moon,—
        The moon,
They danced by the light of the moon.

                —*Edward Lear.*

A Lobster Quadrille

"Will you walk a little faster?" said a
    whiting to a snail;
"There's a porpoise close behind us,
    and he's treading on my tail.
See how eagerly the lobsters and the
    turtles all advance!
They are waiting on the shingle—will
    you come and join the dance?
Will you, won't you, will you, won't you,
    will you join the dance?
Will you, won't you, will you, won't you,
    won't you join the dance?

"You can really have no notion how
    delightful it will be,
When they take us up and throw us,
    with the lobsters, out at sea!"
But the snail replied, "Too far, too far!"
    and gave a look askance—

Said he thanked the whiting kindly,
    but he would not join the dance:
Would not, could not, would not,
    could not, would not join the dance;
Would not, could not, would not,
    could not, could not join the dance.

"What matters it how far we go?" his
    scaly friend replied,
"There is another shore, you know,
    upon the other side.
The further off from England,
    the nearer is to France—
Then turn not pale, beloved snail, but
    come and join the dance:
Will you, won't you, will you, won't you,
    will you join the dance?
Will you, won't you, will you, won't you,
    won't you join the dance?"

                        —*Lewis Carroll.*

The Mountain and the Squirrel

The mountain and the squirrel
Had a quarrel,
And the former called the latter
    "Little Prig."
Bun replied:
"You are doubtless very big:
But all sorts of things and weather
Must be taken in together
To make up a year
And a sphere;
And I think it no disgrace
To occupy my place.
If I'm not so large as you,
You are not so small as I,
And not half so spry.
I'll not deny you make
A very pretty squirrel track;
Talents differ; all is well and wisely
    put;
If I cannot carry forests on my back,
Neither can you crack a nut!"

—Ralph Waldo Emerson.

Tom the Chimney-Sweep

Once upon a time there was a little chimney-sweep named Tom. He lived in a great town in the north country, where there were plenty of chimneys to sweep. Tom could not read nor write, and did not care to do either. He never washed himself, for there was no water where he lived. He cried half his time and laughed the other half. He cried when he had to climb the dark chimneys and got the soot into his eyes, which he did every day in the week. He cried when his master beat him, which he did every day in the week. He cried when he had not enough to eat, which happened every day in the week. And he laughed the other half of the day, when he was tossing pennies with the boys, or playing leap-frog over the posts, or rolling stones at horses as they trotted by.

One day a smart little groom rode into

the court where Tom lived. He wanted Mr. Grimes to come the next morning to his master's house, for the chimneys needed sweeping.

Now, Mr. Grimes was Tom's master, so he and Tom set out early next morning. Grimes rode the donkey in front, while Tom and the brushes walked behind.

They passed through the village and through the turnpike, and then they were out in the real country on the black dusty road.

On they went. Tom longed to get over the gate and pick buttercups and look for birds' nests; but Grimes was a man of business and would not hear of that.

Soon they came up to a poor Irishwoman, with a bundle on her back. She had a gray shawl over her head and she wore a red petticoat. She had neither shoes nor stockings, and limped along as if she were tired. She was a tall, handsome woman, with bright gray eyes and heavy black hair hanging about her cheeks. She walked

beside Tom and talked to him, and asked him where he lived and what he knew and all about himself.

Then Tom asked her where she lived, and she said far away by the sea. He asked her about the sea, and she told him how it rolled and roared over the rocks in winter nights and how it lay still in bright summer days for the children to bathe and play in. Tom longed to go to the sea and to bathe in it.

At last at the bottom of a hill they came to a stream of clear water. Tom ran down to the stream and began washing his face. "Come along," said Grimes. "What do you want with washing yourself?"

"Those that wish to be clean, clean they will be, and those that wish to be foul, foul they will be," said the Irishwoman. "You will see me again." And she turned away.

Tom rushed after her, shouting, "Come back!" But when he got into the meadow the woman was not there.

When Grimes and Tom had gone three miles and more they came to a long avenue of trees. Tom had never seen such great trees, and as he looked up he thought that the blue sky rested on their heads. When they came to the grand old house, Tom wondered how many chimneys were in it.

The housekeeper met them and gave the orders. Grimes listened and said every now and then under his voice, "Mind that, you little beggar." Then the housekeeper turned them into a grand room, all covered with sheets and brown paper. She bade them begin and, after a whimper or two and a kick from his master, into the grate Tom went, and up the chimney.

How many chimneys he swept I cannot say, but he swept so many that he got very tired and lost his way in them. He came down the wrong chimney and found himself standing on a rug in a strange room.

Tom looked about. He thought the room was very pretty. It was all in white. There were white window-curtains, white bed-curtains, white furniture and white walls, with a little pink here and there. The carpet was gay with little flowers and the wall was hung with pictures.

The next thing he saw was a washstand, with soap, brushes and towels, and a large bath tub full of clean water. "She must be a very dirty lady," thought Tom, "to need so much water." Then he looked toward the bed and there he saw the lady and he held his breath.

Under the snow-white cover, upon the

snow-white pillow, lay the most beautiful little girl Tom had ever seen. He looked at her pretty skin and golden hair, and wondered whether she was a real person or one of the wax dolls he had seen in the shops. When he saw her breathe he made up his mind that she was alive, and he stood staring at her as if she had been an angel.

"She cannot be dirty. She never could have been dirty," thought Tom to himself. Then he thought, "Are all people like that when they are washed?" He looked at his own wrist and tried to rub the soot off and wondered whether it would come off.

He looked around and saw, standing close to him, a little black ragged boy. "What are you doing here?" he cried. Then he saw that it was himself in a great mirror.

So Tom, for the first time in his life, found out that he was dirty. He burst into tears and turned to go up the chimney again and hide, but he upset the fender and threw the fire irons down with a noise as of ten thousand tin kettles tied to ten thousand dogs' tails.

Up jumped the little white lady in her bed and screamed. The old nurse rushed in from the next room and, seeing Tom, thought that he had come to rob. She dashed at him and caught him by the jacket, but she did not hold him. He doubled under the good woman's arm and was out of the window in a moment.

The gardener saw him and gave chase to poor Tom. The dairymaid heard the noise and she jumped up and gave chase. Grimes upset the soot sack and he ran out and gave chase. The plowman left his horses and gave chase. The Irishwoman saw Tom and she gave chase, too.

Tom made for the woods. But the boughs laid hold of his legs and arms, poked him in the face and stomach and made him shut his eyes tight. "I must get out of this," thought Tom, "or they will catch me."

Suddenly he ran his head against a wall. Up he went and over that like a squirrel.

There Tom was, out on the great moor. He ran along the wall for nearly half a mile.

The gardener and the plowman and the dairymaid went on half a mile the other way, inside the wall. But the Irishwoman had watched which way Tom went. So she went over the wall and followed him.

Little Tom stared about the strange place. It was like a new world to him. He saw great spiders, with crowns and crosses on their backs, sitting in the middle of their webs. He saw lizards, brown and gray and green, and he thought they were snakes, and would sting him; but they were as much frightened as he was.

Tom went on and on, he hardly knew why; but he liked the great strange place and the cool fresh air.

"What a big place the world is!" he said, for now he could see dark woods and great plains and farms and villages, and far below he could see a clear stream of water. Tom thought he could get down there in five minutes, so down, down he went.

At last he came to a bank of beautiful shrubs. He lay down on the grass, but he did not fall asleep. He turned and tossed and felt so hot all over that he longed to get into the river to cool off. He went to the bank, and looked into the clear water. Every pebble was bright and clean, and the silver trout dashed off in fright at the sight of his black face. Tom dipped his hand in and felt it cooled, and said, "I will be a fish, I will swim in the water, I must be clean, I must be clean."

He put his hot sore feet into the water,

then his legs, and then he went far in.

All the while Tom never saw the Irishwoman coming down behind him. She, too, stepped into the cool water, her shawl and her petticoat faded away, the green water-weeds floated round her sides. The white waterlilies floated round her head. The fairies of the stream came up from the bottom and bore her down in their arms, for she was their queen.

"Where have you been?" they asked her.

"I have been nursing sick folks; and whispering sweet dreams into their ears. I have been doing all that I can to help those who will not help themselves; and I have brought you a little brother." Then all the fairies laughed for joy. But the fairy queen said, "He is a little savage now and like the beasts, and from the beasts he must learn. So you must not play with him, nor speak to him, nor let him see you. You must only keep him from harm."

Then the fairies were sad because they could not play with their new brother, but they always did what they were told. And the queen floated down the river.

Tom tumbled himself into the clear, cool stream. He had not been in it two minutes before he fell fast asleep, and dreamed about the green meadows and the elm trees and the sleeping cows. When he awoke he was swimming about in the stream. He was only four inches long now, and he had a set of gills round his neck. The fairies had turned Tom into a water-baby.

—*Arranged from Charles Kingsley's "Water Babies."*

Tom the Water-Baby

For the first time in his life, Tom felt how comfortable it was to have nothing on him. He was very happy in the water. He had nothing to do now but enjoy himself, and look at all the pretty things in the water-world, where the sun is never too hot and the frost is never too cold.

Sometimes he swam along, looking at the crickets which ran in and out over the stones. Sometimes he climbed over the rocks and watched the sandpipers running about. Then sometimes he came to a water-forest. There in the water-forest he saw the water-monkeys and water-squirrels with six legs. Almost every thing in the water has six legs except elves and water-babies.

There were water-flowers too, and Tom saw that they were alive and busy. He soon learned to understand them and talk to them. He might have had very pleasant company if he only had been a good boy. But he pecked the poor water-things about till they were afraid of him, and got out of his way or crept into their shells. So he had no one to speak to or to play with.

One day Tom came to a pool of little trout. He began teasing them and trying to catch them, but they slipped through his fingers and jumped clear out of the water in their fright. As Tom chased them he came close to a great dark hole. Out jumped a creature with six legs, a big stomach, and a big head, with two great eyes and a face like a donkey's.

"Oh," said Tom, "you are an ugly fellow," and he began making faces at it. He put his nose close to it and shouted at it. Then the donkey-face came off and out popped a long arm, with a pair of pincers at the end of it, and caught Tom by the nose. It did not hurt him much, but it held him tight.

"Oh, let me go!" cried Tom.

"Then let me go," said the creature. "I want to be quiet. I want to split."

Tom promised to let it go. "But why do you want to split?" he asked.

"Because my brothers and sisters have all split and turned into beautiful creatures with wings. I want to split, too. Don't speak to me. I am sure I shall split. I will split."

Then the creature swelled and puffed, and stretched out stiff, and at last split down the back, and then up to its head. Out came the most slender soft creature, but it was very pale and weak. It moved its legs feebly and looked about. Then it began walking slowly up a grass stem to the top of the water.

Tom stared with all his eyes. Then he went up to the top of the water and peeped out to see what would happen. As the creature sat in the warm bright sun, a wonderful change came over it. It grew strong and firm. The most lovely colors began to show on its body, blue and yellow and black, spots and bars and rings. From its back rose four great wings of bright gauze. Its eyes grew so large that they filled all its head and shone like diamonds.

"Oh, you beautiful creature!" said Tom, and he put out his hand to catch it. But the thing flew up in the air and then settled down again on Tom, quite fearlessly.

"You cannot catch me," it said. "I am a dragon-fly now. I am the king of all the flies. I shall dance in the sunshine and catch gnats." And he flew away into the air.

"Oh! Come back, come back," cried Tom, "you beautiful creature! I have no one to play with and I am so lonely here. If you will come back I will never try to catch you," and Tom wished that he could change his skin and have wings.

One day Tom had a new adventure. He was sitting on a water-leaf with his friend the dragon-fly, watching the gnats dance. The dragon-fly had eaten as many as he wanted and was sitting quite still and sleepy, for it was hot and bright.

Suddenly Tom heard the strangest noise up the stream. He took a neat little header into the water and started off to see what it was. When he came near, he saw four or five beautiful creatures. They were many times larger than Tom and were swimming about, rolling and diving in the most charming way.

When the biggest one saw Tom, she cried, "Quick, children! Here is something to eat." She came to poor Tom and looked at him with such wicked eyes that he slipped down between the water-lily roots as fast as he could. Then he turned round and made faces at her.

"Come out," said the wicked old otter, "or it will be worse for you."

But Tom looked at her from between two thick roots and shook them with all his might, making faces all the time.

"Come away, children," said the otter, "it is not worth eating. It is only an elf; we do not eat elves."

"I am not an elf!" said Tom.

"I say you are an elf, and therefore you are, and not good food for me and my children. You may stay there till the salmon eat you."

"What are salmon?" asked Tom.

"Fish, nice fish to eat. They are the lords of the fish, and we are the lords of the salmon," and she laughed again. "We hunt them up and down the pools and drive them into a corner. They bully the little trout and the minnows till they see us coming. Then they are afraid and we catch them."

"And where do the salmon come from?" asked Tom, for it was all very strange to him.

"They come out of the sea, the great wide sea, where they might stay and be safe if they would. But out of the sea the silly things come into the river, and we come up to watch for them."

Then the otter swam away and Tom saw her no more for that time. But he kept thinking of what the otter had said about the great river and the sea, and he longed to go to see them. He thought about it all day.

Suddenly it grew dark. Tom looked up and saw black clouds above his head. He did not feel frightened but he kept quiet, for everything was still. There was not a whisper of wind, nor a chirp of a bird to be heard. Next a few drops of rain fell into the water, and one hit Tom on the nose and made him pop his head down.

Then the thunder roared and the lightning flashed from cloud to cloud. Tom looked up through the water and thought it was the finest thing that he had ever seen. But out of the water he dared not put his head, for the rain came down so hard. Tom

could hardly stand against the stream, so he hid behind a rock.

Then the otter came sweeping along. She saw Tom and said, "Now is the time, elf, if you want to see the world. Come along, children. We shall breakfast on salmon tomorrow. Down to the sea, down to the sea!"

Then came a flash of lightning brighter than all the rest. By the light of it Tom saw three beautiful little babies with their arms around one another floating down the stream. They sang, "Down to the sea, down to the sea!"

"Wait for me!" cried Tom, but they were gone. Yet he could hear them singing, "Down to the sea."

"Down to the sea!" said Tom. "Everything is going to the sea, and I will go too."

So down the rushing stream went Tom, past sleeping villages, under dark bridges, and away to the sea. After a while he came to a place where the river spread out, and there he stopped. "This must be the sea," he thought. "I will stop here and look out for the otter or the eels or someone to tell me where to go."

So he went back a little way and crept into the crack of a rock. There he waited and slept, for he was tired with his journey. When he awoke the stream was clear. After awhile, he saw a sight which made him jump. It was a fish ten times as big as the biggest trout. Such a fish!—shining silver from head to tail, with here and there a crimson dot, with a hooked nose and a great bright eye. It looked around as proudly as a king. "Surely he must be the salmon, the king of all the fish," thought Tom.

Tom was frightened, but the salmon looked him full in the face and then went on. With a swish or two of its tail the salmon made the stream boil. In a few minutes another came, and then four or five, and so on. They all passed Tom, now and then leaping out of the water and over a rock. At last one bigger than all the rest came up. He looked at Tom and said, "What do you want here?"

"Oh, don't hurt me!" cried Tom. "I only want to look at you. You are so handsome."

"Ah!" said the salmon, "I see what you are, my little dear. I have met one or two creatures like you before and I have found them kind and well-behaved."

"So you have seen things like me before?" asked Tom.

"Several times, my dear. Indeed, it was only last night that one came and warned me of some new nets in the stream."

"So there are babies in the sea?" cried Tom, and he clapped his hands. "Then I shall have some one to play with me there?"

"Were there no babies up the stream?" asked the salmon.

"No," said Tom, "I thought I saw three last night; but they went down to the sea. So I went too, for I had nothing to play with but dragon-flies."

Then Tom told the salmon about the wicked otter and warned him to watch out. Soon the salmon went on up the river and Tom went slowly along the shore, led by the fairies whom he never saw. On and on he went.

All at once the water, which had been fresh, turned salt all round him. Then there came a change over Tom. He felt strong and light and fresh. He gave three skips out of the water a yard high, head over heels, just as the salmon do when they first touch the salt water.

A red buoy was dancing in the open sea, and to the buoy Tom went. He passed great shoals of bass and mullet, rushing after the shrimps. Once he passed a great black seal, who was coming in after the mullet. The seal put his head and shoulders out of the water and stared at Tom, looking like a fat old man with a gray head. Instead of being frightened, Tom said, "How do you do, sir? What a beautiful place the sea is!"

The old seal looked at him with his soft, sleepy eyes and said, "Good-tide to you, my little man. Are you looking for your brothers and sisters? I passed them all at play outside."

"Oh," said Tom, "then I shall have play-fellows at last!" and he swam to the buoy, and got upon it, and looked around for water-babies. Sometimes he thought he saw them at the bottom of the sea, but it was only the pink and white shells. Once he was sure he had found one, for he saw two bright eyes peeping out of the sand. So he dived down and began to scrape the sand away. "Don't hide," he cried, "I do want some one to play with me."

To have come all this way and yet to find no water-babies! It did seem hard. So Tom sat down on the bottom of the sea and cried salt tears.

For days and weeks Tom sat upon the buoy, looking out to sea, and wondering when the water-babies would come back. Yet they never came. He began to ask all the strange things that came from the sea if they had seen any water-babies. Some said, "Yes," and some said nothing at all.

There came a fleet of purple sea-snails floating along, each on a sponge full of foam. Tom said, "Where do you come from, you pretty creatures? Have you seen the water-babies?"

The sea-snails answered, "Yes, we have seen the water-babies. We have seen many strange things as we sailed along." And they floated away.

Then there came some porpoises, rolling as they went—papas and mammas, and little children—all smooth and shiny.

Tom spoke to them. All they answered was, "Hush, hush, hush!" for that was all they had learned to say.

Then there came some sharks, many of them as long as a boat, and Tom was frightened. But they were lazy, good-natured fellows. They came and rubbed their great sides against the buoy, and lay in the sun with their back fins out of the water and winked at Tom, but he never could get them to speak.

Next there came a beautiful creature like a ribbon of pure silver, with a sharp head and long teeth, but it seemed sick and sad.

"I have come north from the warm sand banks," it said. "I met some ice-bergs in the ocean. I was caught among them and chilled. But the water-babies helped me and set me free. Now I am getting better every day."

"Oh!" cried Tom, "you have seen the water-babies? Have you seen any near here?"

"Yes, they helped me again last night or I should have been eaten by a great black porpoise."

Tom now left the buoy and went along the sands and round the rocks and cried and called for the water-babies, but he heard no voice in return. At last, with his fretting and crying, he grew quite lean and thin.

One day among the rocks he found a play-fellow. It was not a water-baby. It was a lobster. Tom had never seen a lobster before and he was greatly taken with this one. The lobster had one claw knobbed and the other jagged. He held on to the seaweed with his knobbed claw, while he cut up salads with his jagged one. Then he put them into his mouth, after smelling at them like a monkey.

If he wanted to go into a narrow crack ten yards off, what do you think he did? He turned his tail to it and laid his long horns straight down his back to guide him, and away he went, pop, into the hole. Then he

peeped out and twiddled his whiskers as much as to say, "You couldn't do that."

Tom asked the lobster about the water-babies. "Yes," he said, "I have seen them often but I do not think much of them. They are meddlesome little creatures that go about helping fish and shells. For my part, I would be ashamed to be helped by little soft creatures that have not even a shell on their backs."

The lobster was a surly old fellow and

not very civil to Tom. But he was so funny, and Tom was so lonely, that they did not quarrel. They used to sit in holes in the rocks and chat for hours.

One day, when Tom was going along the rocks, he saw a round cage. In it sat his friend the lobster twiddling his horns and looking very much ashamed of himself.

"Have you been naughty, and have they put you into the lock-up?" asked Tom.

"I can't get out," said the lobster.

"Why did you get in?"

"After that piece of dead fish."

"Where did you get in?"

"Through the round hole at the top."

"Then why don't you get out through it?"

"Because I can't. I have jumped upward, and downward, and backward, and sideways, at least four thousand times. I can't get out. I can't find the hole." And the lobster twiddled his horns and looked at Tom.

Tom looked at the trap and, having more wit than the lobster, he saw what was the matter. "Stop a bit," said Tom. "Turn your tail up to me, and I will pull you through hind foremost. Then you won't stick in the spikes." But the lobster was so clumsy that he could not find the hole.

Tom reached in till he caught hold of him, and then the lobster pulled Tom in head first.

"Hello! here is a pretty business," said Tom. "Now take your great claws and break the points off the spikes. Then we shall both get out easily."

"Dear me, I never thought of that!" said the lobster. But they had not broken half the spikes when they saw a dark cloud over them. It was the otter.

How she did grin and grin when she saw Tom. "You little meddlesome wretch, I have you now! I will punish you for telling the salmon where I was," said she, and she crawled all over the pot to get in.

Tom was frightened when the otter

found the hole in the top and squeezed through it. But no sooner was her head inside than the lobster caught her by the nose and held on.

There they were, all three in the pot, rolling over and over, and very tight packing it was. The lobster tore at the otter, and the otter tore at the lobster, and both squeezed and thumped poor Tom till he had no breath left in his body. I don't know what would have happened to him if he had not at last got on the lobster's back and out of the hole.

He was glad when he got out, but he would not desert his friend. The first time he saw the lobster's tail uppermost he caught hold of it and pulled with all his might. But the lobster would not let go of the otter.

"Come along," said Tom, "don't you see she is dead?"

But the lobster would not let go.

"Come along, or the fisherman will catch you!" and that was true, for Tom felt someone hauling up the pot. But still the lobster would not let go of the otter. Tom saw the fisherman haul the lobster to the side of the boat, and thought it was all up with him. But when the lobster saw the fisherman, he gave a furious snap, and slipped out of his hand and out of the pot and safe into the sea; but he left his knobbed claw behind him.

And now a most wonderful thing happened to Tom. He had not left the lobster five minutes before he came upon a water-baby. It was a real live water-baby sitting on the sand. Now, was it not strange that Tom could never find a water-baby till after he had helped the lobster?

When the water-baby saw Tom, it looked up for a moment and then cried, "Why, you are not one of us! You are a new baby." It ran to Tom, and Tom ran to it, and they hugged and kissed each other for ever so long.

At last Tom said, "Oh, where have you been all this while? I have been looking for you so long, and I have been so lonely."

"We have been here for days and days. There are hundreds of us among the rocks. How was it you did not see us or hear us? We sing and romp every evening before we go home."

Tom looked at the baby again and then he said, "Well, this is wonderful! I have seen things just like you again and again, but I thought you were shells or sea creatures. I never thought you were water-babies like myself."

Then Tom heard the other babies

coming, laughing and singing and shouting and romping. The noise they made was just like the noise of the ripples. So he knew that he had been hearing and seeing the water-babies all the time, only he did not know them because his eyes and ears were not opened.

When the tide began to turn, in came the water-babies. Some were bigger and some were smaller than Tom, all in the neatest little white bathing dresses. When they found that Tom was a new baby, they put him in the middle and danced around him on the sand. Little Tom was as happy as he could be.

"We have mended all the broken sea-weed, and put all the rocks in order, and planted all the shells again in the sand. Nobody will see where the ugly storm swept in last week. And now," they all cried at once, "we must come away home! We must come away home!"

—Arranged from Charles Kingsley's "Water Babies."

Tom Becomes a Man

Tom was delighted with the home of the water-babies, which was on an island full of caves. There were blue caves and white caves draped with seaweed, purple and crimson, green and brown; and there was soft white sand where the water-babies slept every night. The rocks were covered with ten thousand anemones and corals, which kept the water clean and pure. The fairies dressed them in the most beautiful colors and patterns, till they looked like great flower-beds.

But Tom did not give up teasing the sea creatures. He frightened the crabs to make them hide in the sand and peep out at him. He put stones into the anemones' mouths to make them think their dinner was coming. The other children warned him and said, "Take care what you do. Mrs. Be-done-by-as-you-did is coming." But Tom never heeded them. One Friday morning Mrs. Be-done-by-as-you-did came. She had on a black bonnet and a black shawl,

and a pair of large green spectacles. She had a hooked nose, and under her arm she carried a birch rod. She was so ugly that Tom wanted to make faces at her, but he was afraid of the birch rod under her arm.

When the children saw her, they stood in a row, and put their hands behind them. She looked at them one by one and gave them all sorts of nice sea things—sea-cakes, sea-apples and sea-oranges.

Little Tom watched all these sweet

things till his mouth watered, and his eyes grew as round as an owl's. He hoped that his turn would come soon, and so it did. The lady called Tom up and held something in her fingers, and popped it into his mouth. But lo and behold, it was a cold, hard pebble!

"You are a cruel woman," said Tom, and he began to cry.

"And you are a cruel boy to put pebbles into the sea-anemones' mouths. As you did to them, so I must do to you."

"Who told you that?" said Tom.

"You did yourself, this very minute."

Tom had never opened his lips, so he was very much surprised.

"Yes, every one tells me exactly what he has done, and that without knowing it. There is no use trying to hide anything from me. Now go, and be a good boy, and I will put no more pebbles into your mouth."

"I did not know there was any harm in it," said Tom.

"Then you know now," said she. "The lobster did not know there was any harm in the lobster pot, but it caught him all the same."

"Dear me," thought Tom, "she knows everything!" And so she did. "Well, you are a little hard on a poor lad," he said.

"Not at all. I am the best friend you ever had in all your life. I only punish people when they do wrong. I like it no more than they do. I am often sorry for them, poor things!" And the strange fairy smiled at Tom and said, "You thought me very ugly just now, did you not?"

Tom hung down his head, and grew very red about the ears.

"I am ugly. I am the ugliest fairy in the world and I shall be, till people behave themselves. Then I shall grow as handsome as my sister, who is the loveliest fairy in the world. Her name is Mrs. Do-as-you-would-be-done-by. She begins where I end and I begin where she ends. Those who will not listen to her, must listen to me, as you will see. And now be a good boy, and do as you would be done by. And when my sister, Mrs. Do-as-you-would-be-done-by, comes, she will take notice of you," and the fairy went away.

One morning Mrs. Do-as-you-would-be-done-by came. All the little children began dancing and clapping their hands, and Tom danced too with all his might. As for the pretty lady, Tom could not tell the color of her hair or her eyes. When he looked at her, he thought she had the sweetest, kindest face he had ever seen. She understood babies and she loved to play with them. When the children saw her, they all caught hold of her, and pulled her till she sat down on a stone. Then they climbed into her lap, and clung round her neck, and caught hold of her hands. Those who could get no nearer, sat on the sand at her feet. Tom stood staring at them, for he could not understand what it was all about.

"Who are you, my little darling?" she asked.

"Oh, this is the new baby!" they all cried, "and he never had any mother."

"Then I will be his mother, and he shall have the best place." So she took Tom into her arms and kissed him, and patted him, and talked to him, and Tom looked up and loved her. Then he fell fast asleep. When he awoke she was telling the children a story.

"Now," said the fairy to Tom, "will you be a good boy and torment no more beasts?"

Tom promised to be a good boy, and he did not tease the sea-beasts after that.

So this fairy taught Tom to do as he would be done by. She taught him to go where he did not like to go, and to help someone that he did not like. This was hard for Tom, and he said, "You want me to go after that horrid old Grimes. I don't like him and, if I find him, he will turn me into a chimney-sweep again."

"Come here, and see what happens to people who do only what is pleasant," said the fairy. She showed a book full of pictures of Do-as-you-likes. They had left the country of Hardwork because they wanted to play all day long, and do only what they liked.

When Tom came to the end of the book he looked sad. The fairy turned to him and said, "My dear, they should have behaved like men, and they should have done what they did not like. The longer they waited and behaved like beasts, the more like them they grew. You came very near being turned into a beast once or twice, little

Tom. Indeed, if you had not made up your mind to go to see the world like a man, you might have ended as an elf in a pond."

"Oh, dear me!" said Tom, "sooner than that, I'll go to the end of the world to find Grimes."

"Ah!" said the fairy, "that is a brave, good boy. But you must go further than that if you want to find Mr. Grimes. He is at the Other-end-of-nowhere."

So away Tom went for days and months, asking all he met if they had seen Mr. Grimes. At last he came to the great iron door of a prison. Tom knocked at the door.

"Who is there?" asked a deep voice.

"If you please, sir, I want to see Mr. Grimes."

"Grimes? He is the most hard-hearted fellow I have in charge. He is up chimney number 345. You will have to go to the roof."

As Tom walked along the dirty roof, he

was surprised to see that the soot did not stick to his feet or make them dirty. At last he came to chimney number 345. Out of the top of it stuck poor Mr. Grimes. He was sooty and ugly, and in his mouth was a pipe.

Grimes looked up and said, "Why it's Tom! I suppose, Tom, you have come to laugh at me."

"No," said Tom, "I only want to help you."

"I do not want anything except a light to this pipe, and that, I can't get," said Grimes.

"I'll get you one," said Tom. He took up a live coal and put it to Grimes' pipe, but it went out instantly.

"But can't I help you in any other way? Can't I help you to get out of this chimney?" asked Tom.

"No, it is no use," said Grimes, "I get nothing I ask for. Did I ask to sweep these chimneys? Did I ask to stick fast in the very first chimney because it was so full

of soot? Did I ask to stay here a hundred years and never get my pipe nor anything fit for a man?"

"No," answered a voice behind. "Neither did Tom ask it when you behaved to him in the same way."

It was Mrs. Be-done-by-as-you-did. Tom made a low bow.

"Oh, Ma'am," said Tom, "don't think about me. That is all past and gone, but may I not help poor Mr. Grimes? May I try to get some of these bricks away so that he can move his arms?"

"You may try, of course," said the fairy, and she disappeared.

For a long time Tom pulled and tugged at the bricks, but he could not move one. Then he tried to wipe Mr. Grimes' face, but the soot would not come off. "Oh, dear!" he said, "I have come all this way to help you, and now I am of no use after all."

"You had best leave me alone," said Grimes. "You are a forgiving little chap, and that's the truth; but you had better be off. The hail is coming soon and it will beat the eyes out of your little head."

"What hail?" said Tom.

"Hail that falls here every evening. Till it comes close to me it's like warm rain. Then it turns to hail over my head and hits me like small shot. So you go along, you kind little chap, and don't look at a man crying, that's old enough to be your father. I am beat now, and beat I must be. 'Foul I would be and foul I am,' as an Irishwoman said to me once. It is all my own fault, but it is too late." And he cried so bitterly that Tom began crying too.

As poor Grimes cried, his tears washed the soot off his face and off his clothes. Then they washed the mortar away from between the bricks. The chimney crumbled down, and Grimes began to get out of it.

"Will you obey me, if I give you a chance?" asked the fairy, returning suddenly.

"I beg pardon, Ma'am, but I never disobeyed you that I know of. I never had the honor of setting eyes upon you till I came to this place," said Grimes.

"Never saw me? Who said to you, 'Those that will be foul, foul they will be?'"

Grimes looked up, and Tom looked up too. It was the Irishwoman who met them the day they went into the country. "I gave you warning then," said she. "Every bad word that you said, every cruel and mean thing that you did, every time that you got tipsy, every day that you went dirty, you were disobeying me, whether you knew it or not."

"If I had only known, Ma'am!" said Grimes.

"You knew well enough that you were disobeying something. But, come out and take your chance."

So Grimes stepped out of the chimney, and looked as clean as a man need look.

"Take him away;" said she to the keeper, "and give him his ticket-of-leave."

"Now," said the fairy to Tom, "your work here is done. You may as well go back again."

"I should be glad to go," said Tom, "but how am I to get out of this place?"

"I will take you out, but first I must bandage your eyes," she said. So the fairy tied the bandage over his eyes with one hand, and with the other she took it off.

Tom opened his eyes very wide, for he thought he had not moved a single step. He looked around him and the first thing he saw was a lovely little creature looking down from a rock where she was sitting. When he came close to her, she looked up and said, "Why, I know you! You are the little chimney-sweep who came into my room."

"Dear me!" cried Tom, "I know you, too. You are the little lady of the white room. How you have grown!"

"And how you have grown, too!" said she.

Then they heard the fairy say, "Attention, children!" They looked up and there stood the Irishwoman. She looked so beautiful that Tom was delighted. She smiled and turned to the little girl and said, "You may take him home with you, Elsie. He has won his spurs in the great battle because he has done the thing he did not like to do." So Tom went home with Elsie.

Tom is now a great man of science. He can plan railroads, he can make steam engines, he can build electric telegraphs, and he knows everything about everything. All this he learned when he was a water-baby under the sea.

—*Arranged from Charles Kingsley's "Water Babies."*

A Boy's Song

Where the pools are bright and deep,
Where the gray trout lies asleep,
Up the river and o'er the lea,
That's the way for Billy and me.

Where the blackbird sings the latest.
Where the hawthorn blooms the sweetest,
Where the nestlings chirp and flee,
That's the way for Billy and me.

Where the mowers mow the cleanest,
Where the hay lies thick and greenest,
Where to trace the homeward bee,
That's the way for Billy and me.

Where the hazel bank is steepest,
Where the shadow falls the deepest,
Where the clustering nuts fall free,
That's the way for Billy and me.

Why the boys should drive away
Little sweet maidens from the play,
Or love to banter and fight so well,
That's the thing I never could tell.

But this I know, I love to play,
Through the meadow, among the hay;
Up the water and o'er the lea,
That's the way for Billy and me.

—James Hogg.

How the Leaves Came Down

I'll tell you how the leaves came down,
    The great Tree to his children said,
"You're getting sleepy, Yellow and Brown,
    Yes, very sleepy, little Red;
    It is quite time you went to bed."

"Ah!" begged each silly, pouting leaf,
    "Let us a little longer stay;
Dear Father Tree, behold our grief,
    'Tis such a very pleasant day
    We do not want to go away."

So, just for one merry day
    To the great Tree the leaflets clung,
Frolicked and danced and had their way,
    Upon the autumn breezes swung,
    Whispering all their sports among,

"Perhaps the great Tree will forget
    And let us stay until the spring,

If we all beg and coax and fret."
    But the great Tree did no such thing;
    He smiled to hear their whispering.

"Come, children all, to bed," he cried;
    And ere the leaves could urge their prayer
He shook his head, and far and wide,
    Fluttering and rustling everywhere,
    Down sped the leaflets through the air.

I saw them; on the ground they lay,
    Golden and red, a huddled swarm,
Waiting till one from far away,
    White bedclothes heaped up on her arm,
    Should come to wrap them safe and warm.

The great bare Tree looked down and smiled.
    "Good-night, dear little leaves," he said;
And from below each sleepy child
    Replied, "Good-night," and murmured,
    "It is so nice to go to bed."

—Susan Coolidge.

Sweet and Low

Sweet and low, sweet and low,
    Wind of the western sea,
Low, low, breathe and blow,
    Wind of the western sea!
Over the rolling waters go;
Come from the dying moon, and blow,
    Blow him again to me;
While my little one, while my pretty one,
      sleeps.

Sleep and rest, sleep and rest;
    Father will come to thee soon.
Rest, rest on mother's breast;
    Father will come to thee soon:
Father will come to his babe in the nest;
Silver sails all out of the west,
    Under the silver moon;
Sleep, my little one, sleep, my pretty one,
      sleep!

—Alfred Tennyson.

September

The golden-rod is yellow;
    The corn is turning brown;
The trees in apple orchards
    With fruit are bending down.

The gentian's bluest fringes
    Are curling in the sun;
In dusty pods the milkweed
    Its hidden silk has spun.

The sedges flaunt their harvest
    In every meadow nook;
And asters by the brookside
    Make asters in the brook.

From dewy lanes at morning
    The grapes' sweet odors rise;
At noon the roads all flutter
    With yellow butterflies.

By all these lovely tokens
    September days are here,
With summer's best of weather,
    And autumn's best of cheer.

—Helen Hunt Jackson.

The Wonderful World

Great, wide, beautiful, wonderful World,
With the wonderful water round you
    curled,
And the wonderful grass upon your breast,
World, you are beautifully drest.

The wonderful air is over me,
And the wonderful wind is shaking the tree—
It walks on the water, and whirls the mills,
And talks to itself on the tops of the hills.

You friendly Earth, how far do you go
With the wheat-fields that nod and the
    rivers that flow,
With cities, and gardens, and cliffs, and isles,
And people upon you for thousands of miles?

Ah, you are so great, and I am so small,
I tremble to think of you, World, at all;
And yet, when I said my prayers to-day,
A whisper inside me seemed to say,
"You are more than the Earth, though
    you are such a dot;
You can love and think, and the Earth
    cannot!"

—William Brighty Rand.

The Throstle

"Summer is coming, summer is coming,
    I know it, I know it, I know it;
Light again, leaf again, life again, love
    again,"
    Yes, my wild little Poet.

Sing the new year in under the blue,
    Last year you sang it as gladly;
"New, new, new, new!" Is it then so new
    That you should carol so madly?

"Love again, song again, nest again,
    young again,"
    Never a prophet so crazy!
And hardly a daisy as yet, little friend,
    See there is hardly a daisy.

"Here again, here, here, here, happy
    year!"
    O warble unchidden, unbidden!
Summer is coming, is coming, my dear,
    And all the winters are hidden.

        —*Alfred, Lord Tennyson.*

The Sea

Come, dear children, let us away;
Down and away below!
Now my brothers call from the bay,
Now the great winds shoreward blow,
Now the salt tides seaward flow,
Now the wild horses play,
Champ and chafe and toss in the spray.
   Children dear, let us away
   This way, this way.

—Matthew Arnold.

Ariel's Song

Where the bee sucks, there suck I:
In a cowslip's bell I lie;
There I couch when owls do cry.
On the bat's back I do fly,
After summer merrily:
Merrily, merrily, shall I live now
Under the blossom that hangs on the
    bough.

—William Shakespeare.

Prayer

He prayeth best who loveth best
Both man and bird and beast.

He prayeth best who loveth best
    All things both great and small;
For the dear God who loveth us
    He made and loveth all.

—Samuel Taylor Coleridge.

CPSIA information can be obtained at www.ICGtesting.com
Printed in the USA
BVOW07s0830170713

326179BV00002B/374/P